THE
RAGAN
BROTHERS

D1557916

THE
RAGAN
BROTHERS

JOE WAYNE BRUMETT

TATE PUBLISHING & *Enterprises*

Published by Tate Publishing & Enterprises, LLC
127 E. Trade Center Terrace | Mustang, Oklahoma 73064 USA
1.888.361.9473 | www.tatepublishing.com

Tate Publishing is committed to excellence in the publishing industry. The company reflects the philosophy established by the founders, based on Psalm 68:11,
"The Lord gave the word and great was the company of those who published it."

Book design copyright © 2010 by Tate Publishing, LLC. All rights reserved.
Cover design by Bekah Garibay
Interior design by Lindsay B. Behrens

Published in the United States of America

ISBN: 978-1-61739-850-6
Fiction / Christian / Historical
10.11.29

DEDICATION

To my wife, Martha Ann, for her loving ways as a Christian mother and wife, who has the Spirit of the Lord in her and spreads that Spirit in song and by example.

I dedicate this book to her.

ACKNOWLEDGMENTS

To my nephew, Tom Brumett, who has stood behind me to give me encouragement and financial help.

To my granddaughter, Marti Henry, who has helped me repeatedly with her knowledge of the computer.

To each member of the fine Tate family for their encouragement and patience.

JOHNNY BECOMES A MEMBER OF THE TM RANCH

Johnny Ragan halted his horse at the edge of the Canadian River at Young's Crossing, southwest of Konowa, Oklahoma. He was a young man of eighteen but had been orphaned when he was eleven, following the War between the States, and had been on his own since. He was raw boned, with a six-foot frame, and a life of hard knocks had hardened him beyond his years. He was thin from lack of nourishment, dirty, and unshaven. He needed bathing, clean clothes, as well as a haircut. His stomach was empty and growling, since it'd been almost two days since he used one of his five remaining bullets to kill a jack rabbit that he had roasted slowly over a fire.

He had come to Young's Crossing, as he knew it was a crossing on the Canadian River used by cattlemen pushing their cattle along the Shawnee Trail as they journeyed north, seeking an outlet to sell their cattle. Perhaps—just perhaps—he could find a herd that needed another drover. This sort of work was not new to him, as he had been a drover on two other occasions, but the jobs had petered out at train stations in Kansas.

His mare was a Grulla and was the last of his belongings that had been handed down to him when his mother died. The Sharp's 1863 .54 cal. rifle was heavy but packed a wallop and had a nasty recoil. He had used most of his money from his first trip north to buy the gun from a Yankee ex-soldier. It was wrapped in an oil cloth and tied just to the right of his old saddle. The four remaining paper-patched cartridges, along with the percussion caps, were in his saddlebags.

Johnny had seen the cloud of dust all morning, and he knew this crossing was the destination of the approaching cattle herd. He had sat under a tree for the shade it afforded. Trees, except along this river, were scarce. So he sat and waited hopefully as he watched the herd of Texas longhorns gather on the opposite shore. There were three drovers and a cook, along with a chuck wagon, drawn by four mules.

The crew was alert, for they noticed him waiting for them and were wary, not knowing his intentions. The herd moved anxiously into the water and were soon up to their hips as they drank and cooled off. An old mossy bull was the lead animal and was prodded by the cowboys toward Johnny's side of the river.

Johnny used his Grulla to cut off a stray and run it back to the herd. A drover nodded his thanks but said nothing. Johnny watched as the chuck wagon was prepared for the crossing. There were two large poles, left by other herds, for the purpose to give the chuck wagon more buoyancy. The crew worked at tying the poles to the chuck wagon, and the cook called to his mules as they began their crossing.

The current was stronger in the middle of the river, and the chuck wagon was spun around as the mules attempted to pull and swim at the same time. The chuck wagon was tipping to one side, and there was a cry of alarm from the cook for help.

Johnny urged his Grulla into the current and lassoed the pole on his side of the chuck wagon. He urged his Grulla back to shore and rode around a large cottonwood tree. The rope grew taut, and the tilting chuck wagon was righted. The mules found their footing, and the chuck wagon was brought safely to shore.

The cook continued to sit on the wagon and called his thanks to Johnny. Drovers began to unfasten the poles from the chuck wagon as a middle-aged man rode up to Johnny. "I'm Rex Hammond, ramrod of this outfit. We are taking these TM cattle to market. You looking for work? I need one more drover. You saved us at least a day's time, and I have no idea where we could replace those provisions that are in the chuck wagon. The pay is forty dollars a month and keep."

"My name is Johnny Ragan, and I am looking for a job. I've made a couple trips north as a drover and am familiar with this kind of work," drawled Johnny.

"I saw you use your rope, and your Grulla knew what to do. Welcome aboard! Cook has some soap, and we plan to lay up here while we all get a bath and try to get rid of some of this dust," said Rex.

"Thanks for the job, Mister Hammond," Johnny said.

"Just call me Rex."

The crew was weary from driving cattle, and the dust of the trail had matted their hair and covered their clothing. While the cattle waded in the waters, the drovers stripped their clothing and, using yellow lye soap, began washing their clothing and bathing themselves in the muddy waters.

The cook came to Johnny and asked him if he would like a haircut, and Johnny agreed. The cook had a pair of hand clippers, comb, and scissors, and Johnny sat while the cook cut and combed.

Johnny sat in ragged wet undergarments while his clothes dried. His long, bony body was noticed by the cook and Rex.

"When was the last time you ate, Johnny?" asked Rex.

"Had a rabbit yesterday, sir," answered Johnny.

The cook went into the chuck wagon and reappeared with four biscuits and bacon sandwiches. Johnny devoured the food and thanked the cook.

Rex was looking at the Sharps and asked Johnny if he had plenty of ammunition

"Got four more left," said Johnny.

"Don't want you to shoot that thing around the herd. We all use Winchester 1866 models and 44 caliber. I think the cook might have some bullets and caps that will fit your gun. When we get back to the TM Ranch, the boss may want you to take some target practice, and if you are good enough, you'll get a new Winchester," explained Rex.

"First time that I've heard of anything like that," said Johnny. "You aiming to keep me on after we deliver the cattle in Kansas?"

"It'll be up to you. I'll be watching you, but I feel like you're one of those who came out of the war hurting for something that you didn't do. You got folks?" asked the ramrod.

"Dad was wounded bad at Vicksburg, and his convalescence killed my mom. Dad died right after she did. Uncle took my younger brother and sister, but he told me I was old enough to take care of myself," Johnny said in a matter-of-fact way. "Dad had left a note that said I was to have the mare, but still I had to fight my uncle to keep her. I was eleven but strong for my age."

The cook looked at Johnny. "You're not such a bad-looking young man with your hair cut and the fuzz gone from your face. You smell better too," he said with a grin. "I have a shirt that I've not worn that you can have for saving me back there in that river. I can't swim a lick."

"Thanks," said Johnny as he took off his ragged shirt and put on the clean one.

"Johnny, I want you to ride with me for the first couple of days," said Rex. "I've my own way of doing things and want you to learn my way. We're in Indian country, so be on the lookout for Kiowa, Comanche, or Kiowa Apache. Hold off with that Sharps, 'cause it will terrify the herd and may well cause a stampede. Can you hit anything with that gun?"

"I miss every once in a while after the game gets around eight hundred yards away," said Johnny. Rex looked at the cook, and both men smiled.

"It's been sometime since we've had a deer or antelope, so give Johnny some of those Sharp shells. Johnny, slip out away from the herd and get us some fresh meat." Rex smiled again at the cook.

The cook gave Johnny a full box of cartridges and caps. Johnny rode eastward along the river and hid himself along a deer path, about a half mile from the camp. He tested the wind and got downwind from the trail and sat in the high grass. The wind was blowing, as it always did, but his keen eyes caught the movement of several deer as they approached the river for their evening drink. Johnny estimated the distance at four hundred yards, lifted the back sight, and adjusted the sight slightly. He pulled the first trigger, shifted his finger to the second, and squeezed. The big gun roared, and they plainly heard the shot in the camp.

"I'll give you two to one that he got a deer." The cook grinned at Rex.

"Hope he did, but he'll need to prove it to me," chided Rex.

Johnny lifted the 180-pound buck onto his Grulla and climbed up behind the carcass.

"I'll tell you what," said the cook. "He'll field dress that deer, but if he gets one you clean it, and if he missed it I'll give you a dollar."

"Make it two dollars," said Rex. He turned to his drovers. "Anyone else want in on this?"

"I hate for you to clean that deer for two bucks; I'll put in a dollar," said Slim Wilkins. Andy was broke as usual and just grinned.

The four watched the trail until Johnny came though the high grass and dumped the buck at their feet.

"Well, I'll be! He said he'd been eating only jackrabbit," said Rex.

"Appears to be a lot of game near this river." said Johnny. "Wait, I'll do that!" He was surprised as Rex began to hang the deer from a lower limb of a cottonwood and prepared to skin it.

"Shot it right behind the left front leg. How far away were you from him?" asked the cook.

"'Reckon it was 'bout four hundred yards," said Johnny.

Slim Wilkins, who was the gunman among the outfit, looked at Johnny and then back to Rex. The cook grinned, and Andy laughed out loud. Johnny looked at Andy, and his forehead wrinkled in question.

Quickly Andy spoke up and said, "No harm meant! We just had a little bet, and the boss lost. Where did you learn to shoot like that?"

"I grew up north of San Antonio and always had a gun of some sort. When I bought this big gun, I played with that back sight until I seldom missed. I was always short on shells and went hungry to buy them," informed Johnny.

Rex was skilled in cleaning deer, and it was not long before the task was complete.

"Johnny, you consider yourself our official hunter. I won't bet against you again." He grinned.

The cook cut out some choice pieces of deer meat, got out his fireside oven, and roasted a goodly portion with potatoes, carrots, and onions. Johnny was surprised when Rex bowed his head and offered a prayer of thanksgiving for the food. It was the first time he had heard anyone pray over the food since his mother died. He sat quietly while the cook, Slim, and Andy all said, "Amen!"

He hobbled his horse where the Grulla could get to grass then put his oil cloth on the ground and, using his saddle as a pillow, laid down on his bed roll. Many thoughts went through his head of the hard times that he had endured and of the many times he had slept with an empty stomach, tired and discouraged. His mother had taught him to read, and he had her Bible, which he read and reread. He felt like reading it, but the light was too dim and there were no candles. *Since I can't let Him speak to me through the Bible, I will speak to Him through prayer,* he thought and prayed for each of these men and of the blessing of finding someone who cared for him. He felt that he had found a family again.

•

He jumped slightly, for a hand was pushing to awaken him.

"It's your turn to ride herd. You can use my Winchester, as the boss doesn't want you to shoot that big gun of yours around the herd," said Andy. "My Winchester is fully loaded, and here is a full box of extra shells."

Johnny arose and estimated the time to be about three o'clock. He saddled his Grulla and rode to a slight hill overlooking the herd. In a soft baritone, he began to sing to the sleeping herd.

Rex heard him sing and smiled. Johnny's voice would blend in well with George's tenor. *Melody will love that boy!* Melody McDowell was the boss's wife. Tom and Melody owned the TM Ranch, and when they were all at the hacienda, sometimes Melody played her piano while some of the cowboys, such as George, sang. A sudden slight pang of homesickness caused him to think of Erma, a maid at the hacienda. Erma Hamilton had lost her husband, slain by a half-breed Apache named Juan Garcia. Erma was a very attractive widow, and Rex, as well as a half dozen other TM Ranch cowboys, were interested in her.

Rex wondered what Erma was doing and went to sleep thinking of the charming lady.

He awoke to the smell of coffee, bacon, and biscuits. Slim was dressed and saddling his horse to relieve Johnny riding herd.

Johnny rode toward the approaching cowboy.

"Something's been bothering the herd. Could be a cougar, or it could be a Comanche. I didn't see anything, but several cows turned their heads toward the north just a few minutes ago. There, look!" Slim followed Johnny's eyes and saw several of the cattle looking toward the north.

"I see what you mean. Go round up the crew. This may mean trouble," said Slim. "Being we're this near to the river, it could be deer." Johnny moved his horse toward the camp while Slim watched the cattle.

A crow called, and several birds began to sing as nature awoke to a new morning.

"Rex, something's bothering the cattle, and Slim told me to get the crew out there," said Johnny. Rex, Andy, and the cook saddled quickly and turned their attention to the herd.

The herd was all standing and looking toward the north. Andy's horse whistled, and several horses answered. Winchesters came out of gun boots as the drovers prepared to defend the herd. Slim, near the small hill near the middle of the herd, began firing steadily.

"Fan out!" called Rex. "Put it to them, Slim!"

Several Indians rode into the herd, and the cattle scattered before them.

Rex, Johnny, and the cook began to fire their Winchesters into the oncoming Indians. Andy had two Colt 44's; Johnny still had his Winchester. The gunfire was deadly, and the Indians were quickly driven away.

"Anybody hurt?" called Rex. "That was a hunting party! I believe they were Comanche. Think I saw someone fall! Who got hit?"

"It's Andy. He's back there somewhere, Rex!" called the cook. The TM cowboys turned their horses back toward the area indicated by the cook.

"Rex, of all the bad luck, I got me an arrow right under the rib cage, and it went clear through. It really burns! Help me to sit up!" He coughed twice, and bright red blood came out of his mouth. Small bubbles formed in his mouth, and he inhaled them as he gasped for breath.

"Got a lung!" the cook whispered to Rex.

Slim was pulling Andy's saddle from Andy's horse and propped the wounded cowboy up on it. The cook rode for a saw at the chuck wagon, and Rex held the protruding arrow with two hands while Slim, as gently as possible, sawed the arrowhead off and pulled it back through Andy's body. The wound was wrapped tightly in a bed sheet.

"Of all the no account bad luck! Leave him right there now. Movin' him may cause him to bleed more. Johnny, stay with him while the rest of us round up those cattle that scattered. Watch out for those Indians; they may still be near us. Slim, you put four down! I think Andy got the one who shot him."

Johnny got off his Grulla and knelt by Andy. Andy's eyes were bulging, and his face was red and tormented. It was plain that he could not breathe. Tommy took his scarf and wiped the blood from Andy's mouth.

"Oh God, help me! Andy needs help. Show me what to do," Johnny cried.

"He needs to breathe!" Again he wiped the blood from Andy's mouth, and with the scarf he reached into his mouth and cleared out more blood. *If I can just blow some air in there,* he thought. He gathered air in his own mouth and blew into Andy's. Andy gasped, and a look of surprise lighted Andy's face. Again Johnny wiped blood and blew again. This process was repeated again and again.

"Thanks!" whispered Andy. Johnny sat back on his heels. The blood appeared to be slowing. Every once in a while he whispered for Andy to open his mouth, and Johnny looked for new blood. He blew several times more into Andy's mouth. Andy was going to sleep ... or was he dying? A feeling of helplessness lingered with Johnny.

"Dear Lord, I'm as helpless as I can be. I know not what to do. Help me to continue to do the right thing." Andy was asleep, but his breathing was shallow. His eyes no longer bulged, and the bleeding had slowed and was stopping. The dressing was stained red, but it didn't seem excessive.

"Lord, thank you for hearing my prayer. Please continue to bless Andy," prayed Johnny.

There was gunfire about a mile off, and it was clearly Winchester fire. Slowly it died out, and Johnny stood and watched some of the cattle as they began to drift back from the grasslands to drink at the river. He checked Andy one more time and then rode out among the cattle and drove them back to the river again. He continued this all morning, and right at noon the cattle lifted their heads and looked into the grasslands. Johnny pulled Andy's Winchester and held his Grulla still while there was movement toward the north.

The cook and Slim rode toward him, pushing a good hundred head of cattle.

"How's Andy?" asked the cook.

"He's sleeping," answered Johnny

"You mean he's dead? I knew he was going to die when I saw where that arrow struck him," said Slim. The cook nodded agreement.

"It was a terrible thing to do. We left him with you knowing that we couldn't get him well. I've been upset all morning thinking of you here with him, and him dying," said the cook as he shook his head. "Sorry, Johnny! You're too young to take on that kind of responsibility."

"He's sleeping and has been all morning. I think he's going to make it, if he doesn't tear something loose in there," said Johnny.

The cook looked at Slim, and they slowly climbed down from their horses. Andy was still but had turned over and was now lying on his right side. Both men looked at him and back to Johnny.

"What did you do?" asked the cook. Slim had the same question on his face.

"I prayed! Our God heard my prayer and told me what to do. I kept the blood out of his mouth and blew my breath into his mouth. He couldn't breathe, you see. I worked at this all morning, and Andy began to breathe on his own and the blood cleared up to a degree. Then he went to sleep and was sitting up. I wondered if his lower lungs were all full of blood, so I turned him on one side and then the other. He vomited once, and it really shook me up, but it cleared his air passages, and he went back to sleep."

"I just can't believe it." said the cook, and Slim agreed.

The cattle were again looking toward the north, and Rex came into camp pushing another hundred head of cattle. He sat and counted cattle for a good twenty minutes.

"Believe that we lost maybe twenty-five," he surmised. "Andy dead?" He looked toward Johnny.

"Boss, you wouldn't believe the change in Andy. He'll live, Boss! He'll live!" cried the cook. Rex sat on his horse with open mouth.

"Praise the good Lord! Who'd of believed it?" asked Rex. He turned toward Johnny. "We left you to watch him die. It wasn't the thing to do with you being so young and all. I'm sorry we did you that way."

The cook told the full story to Rex, while Slim sat quietly on his horse. Rex stood over Andy and watched him breathe.

"You're right! I believe we have witnessed a miracle. He'll live, Praise the Lord, he'll live," said Rex. He sat looking from the cook to Johnny and then at Slim.

"Now what will we do?" asked Rex. "I've got this herd to deliver. We can't turn back!" He took Slim to one side, and they talked in soft tones. He came back to Johnny and sat on his horse while Johnny sat quietly on his Grulla.

"That was a wonderful thing that you did, Johnny. We're all happy that Andy's alive. He can't be moved for a couple of weeks, and someone needs to be here to care for him. Will you stay? Slim and the cook are experienced men with cattle, and either would stay with Andy if I asked them. You appear to be the most logical to remain here and look out for him.

The TM Ranch is about a week's drive from here, and Andy can show you the way when he's able. The cook will leave you provisions for a month, and with what you shoot, you all should eat well. Continue to pray to Him for help, and you'll make it fine. You know, Johnny, the good Lord sent you here to help us. I'm a new Christian, and Erma led me to Christ. I'm just learning to trust in Him more each day. I'll write a letter of introduction for you to give to the TM Ranch. Okay?" asked Rex.

"Yes, and may the good Lord bless you," Johnny answered.

Andy was sitting up, and the cook had made some broth, which he fed the cowboy. Andy listened while Rex told him of his plans for Johnny to see him back to the ranch. Andy kept looking at Johnny, and Johnny could see a look of happiness and appreciation in his eyes.

The cook left a pack mule and provisions for a good month for Johnny and Andy. He left ammunition for the Sharp as well as the Winchester. The three men got the herd up and turned them toward the north. A feeling of loneliness was in the minds of both Johnny and Andy as they watched the herd disappear toward the north.

"How are you feeling, Andy?" asked Johnny.

"I feel like I've come out second best in a fight with a grizzly. My chest is bothering me, and I feel feverish."

Johnny put his hand on the cowboy's brow. Usually a couple days after a gun wound fever will set in if there was infection. The brow felt slightly warm but not hot to the touch.

"You been coughing up more blood?" asked Johnny.

"No, but I have an awful taste in my mouth. I'm not sure it's from the wound or from all that air you blew into my mouth," said Andy, smiling.

"Thanks, friend!"

"I'm going to move closer to the river and put up the tent the cook left. The wind blowing as it is may keep the mosquitoes off. Look out when the wind dies," said Johnny. It was the fourth day since the crew had left, and it appeared that Andy had missed most of the infection. Again, Johnny prayed with Andy and thanked Him for His mercy to them. Johnny also got out his Bible and read to Andy whenever possible, and they talked of what Johnny had read. The days moved into a week, and Andy continued to get stronger. Fellowship grew between the two men, and they became like brothers. The game was plentiful around the river, and Johnny left the Winchester with Andy while he carried the Sharp.

It was the first of a new week that Johnny returned from a hunting trip with a nice buck. Suddenly, he was surrounded by Kiowa Indians, and they stood looking down at Andy. Andy was smiling at a tall Indian dressed in buckskin, a loincloth, and leggings. The Indian was speaking in broken English. Johnny kept his hands away from the Winchester and held up his hand as a sign of peace.

"It's okay, Johnny! This is Red Hand, and he is chief of a Kiowa tribe just west of here. The tribe is a friend of the TM Ranch. Amos, one of our crew, is married to Red Hand's sister. Wolf Fang, Red Hand's dad, comes to the ranch, and he and Red Hand hunt quail with our boss, Tom McDowell. Mr. McDowell gave them both shotguns, and they love to hunt with Tom and his two bird dogs. Wolf Fang is getting along in age but is a good Christian, as is Red Hand," said Andy.

Red Hand was listening to the conversation and spoke out in English. "Red Hand is good Christian. Praise the Lord!" Several of the Indian braves cried, "Praise the Lord!"

"Causes to laugh, sister to Red Hand, is married to spiritual man." Red Hand beat his chest. "Praise the Lord!" Red Hand was looking at the Winchester that Johnny held, and then his eye saw the Sharp wrapped in oil cloth. He reached for the gun, and Johnny barely beat him to it. Johnny lifted the gun and untied the bindings, which held it snug against the saddle.

"This is a Sharp 1863 .54 caliber rifle and shoots this shell." Johnny reached for his saddlebag and took out both bullet and caps. Red Hand stepped back, gestured, and grunted.

"Chief Red Hand wants to see you shoot," Andy said, grinning.

Johnny looked up the river for a target. He saw a doe deer, sniffing a scrape up the river. He pointed to the deer, which was a good eight hundred yards away. Johnny lifted the back sight and slid the peep sight down the back sight. The doe had stopped and was smelling the scrape. She squatted and urinated in the middle of the scrape. Lifting her head, she bounded into the grasslands. Johnny slid the .54 caliber shell into the chamber and put the cap in place. He watched the clearing where the scrape was. There was movement in the grass, and a fourteen-point buck stepped into the clearing to check his scrape that he had dug with his sharp hoofs. He smelled her urine and lifted his head straight up.

Johnny pulled the top trigger and took careful aim and pulled the second trigger. The gun exploded with a terrific roar, and a second later there was a flat spat that knocked the deer on his side. He tried to get up but could not and then laid his head between his front legs and died.

Red Hand and his braves uttered words in the Kiowa language. Andy was all smiles. Red hand was very impressed and looked at Johnny in amazement.

"You have done this many times before?" he asked.

"Yes," said Johnny as he started to put the gun back in the oil skins.

Red Hand took the gun from Johnny and looked at it carefully. He pointed to the back sight, and Johnny explained how adjusting the gun for distance required the raising of the front sight, which was done when the back sight was adjusted. Red Hand explained that he had a double barrel shotgun with two barrels and two triggers. He wondered why the gun had two triggers and why the gun did not shoot when the front trigger was pulled. Johnny explained that the first trigger set the tension on the back trigger, so you didn't need to pull the second trigger so hard to shoot the gun.

Two of the braves rode for the deer, and when they returned to camp they had plenty of help skinning the deer and cutting it into pieces.

Red Hand spoke to Andy. "I believe he and his gun will out-shoot Tom McDowell. I've been trying to beat Tom McDowell for several years. Wolf Fang gave up after our first turkey hunt together." He grinned at Andy.

"Johnny is also a believer in Christ; if it were not for his prayers and his breath, I don't believe I would be alive." said Andy. He continued to tell Red Hand about being shot by the arrow and what Johnny had done.

Red Hand looked again at Johnny.

"Is he medicine man?"

"No, but I heard him ask God what to do. I guess God told him, for I'm getting stronger every day. His breath became my breath, and I live just because he breathed life into my lungs," said Andy.

"Praise the Lord!" said Red Hand. Several braves overheard their chief and cried also "Praise the Lord."

"Maybe the great Spirit gave that bullet the wings and guided it to the heart of that deer. We must praise the Lord, for he has given us the food to eat and the great medicine and spiritual man, Johnny," said Red Hand. Andy started to correct Red Hand and then thought better of it and remained silent.

The fire was built up, and the braves danced around the fire and gave thanks in their way to the great Spirit for the life of the deer. They had never seen a deer killed at such a distance and showed honor to Johnny as they did their chief, Red Hand.

Johnny remembered Paul and Barnabas when they were ship-wrecked and how the natives of the island thought of them as being gods. Paul had reminded the natives that he and Barnabas were human beings and not gods. Johnny told the Indians that he was but a man and did not deserve to be looked upon any higher than they looked on their own children. He bowed his head and offered a prayer of thanks for the deer, for his new friends, and that God had heard his prayer and had given Andy renewed health. When he finished his prayer, Johnny said, "Amen!"

Andy said, "Amen!"

Red Hand cried out, "Amen!"

Things were quiet for a minute, and all the braves said, "Amen." Johnny spoke and said, "It means so be it." Several practiced their new English word and added, "Praise the Lord." Johnny smiled and began to eat the deer the Good Lord had provided.

Johnny told Red Hand that he thought Andy was ready to begin the trip back to the TM Ranch and asked if Red Hand would like to travel with them. Red Hand agreed.

They had an early breakfast and broke camp. Red Hand went to the river; well hidden was a birch bark canoe. Andy and four Indians rode the canoe across, and then it was retuned for Red Hand. Most of the braves rode their horses across. The canoe was hidden on the south side of the river, and the entire group began their journey west toward the ranch. Red Hand put out scouts and rode along with Andy and Johnny.

The grasslands were gently rolling hills, and the grass was high on the horses' thighs. The area used by the herd was apparent, and the party generally followed the trail left by the herd. That way, explained Red Hand, "Our tracks are covered." The group made good time the first half of the day, but Andy appeared tired by mid-afternoon, and rests were made especially because of his health. The wound was well healed, but Andy's strength had not fully returned.

The ranch was estimated to be three hundred fifty miles due west, and that was a long ride for anyone, let alone Andy.

Red Hand was in touch with his scouts as they passed through Apache territory. Though he was a distant relative to most of the Apache, he was concerned about passing through their territory.

Johnny asked Red Hand why he was so far east. Red Hand explained that he was following the herd to make sure it had a safe passage through territory owned by the Kiowa and the Kiowa Apache. Tom McDowell had requested safe passage for his herd from Red Hand. Red Hand had met a tribe of Comanche and had fought a short battle with the hunting party. Johnny thought it could well be the same group that had wounded Andy.

Many of the drovers, driving their cattle along the Shawnee trail, had lost half of their cattle to Indians and rustlers. It would not be long before the trail would be shut down as the area became more populated, and settlers became angered by the cattle grazing into their gardens and planted areas.

After two weeks on the trail, Red Hand pointed the TM Ranch out to Johnny. The ranch was set in a sprawling plain, which was peppered with red dots Johnny knew to be Texas Longhorns. There were several paddocks filled with horses, three large barns, a summer kitchen, a spring house, a well house, a black smith shop, and a bunkhouse. Approximately one hundred yards from the bunkhouse was the hacienda, which was a single story adobe dwelling with a pink tile roof. There was a green lawn with boxwoods and a flower garden behind the house. All the buildings were adobe and whitewashed. Johnny sat and looked with amazement at the beauty of the buildings and the vastness of the ranch. It was the largest ranch he had ever seen.

Two cowhands carrying Winchesters rode toward them from a group of trees on a slight hill. "Hello, Red Hand," called one of the cowhands.

Andy smiled. "We ran into a hunting party on the other side of the Canadian, and I took an arrow. I wouldn't have made it except for this young fellow. Amos, George, meet Johnny Ragan. Johnny this is Amos, who is our scout, and George is one of the ramrods around here. George, Rex hired Johnny as a drover and sent him home with me to make sure I got here. I've a letter from Rex." He pulled the wrinkled letter from his saddlebag. George read the letter and told Amos its contents. Amos apparently could not read.

"Welcome, Johnny. I'll take you over to the bunkhouse soon as we get Andy settled down. Red Hand, the boss will be wanting to talk with you, and thank you for getting Andy home." Amos and George led the party toward the bunkhouse area, and while Amos remained with Johnny and Andy, George took Red Hand to the hacienda.

Johnny stood while they put Andy into his bunk. Andy's eyes showed just how tired he was. Andy fell asleep almost immediately.

"The unmade bunks are not taken by anyone. There are sheets and a blanket here in this closet," said George as he left.

Johnny made his bed and was nearly finished when there came a rap at the bunkhouse door, and a very attractive lady entered and went to Andy's bunk, where she stood and looked at him for a few minutes. She turned toward Johnny and began to assist him making his bed.

"I'm Erma Montgomery. I understand that Rex hired you while you all were on the trail. Rex send any note back?"

"Yes, Andy turned the note over to George and Amos," replied Johnny.

There was another rapping at the door, and a very tomboyish young lady came rushing into the bunkhouse. Her eyes were blue, and her braided hair was light brown. She stood looking toward Andy and then turned her attention to Johnny.

"Hi, I'm Cheryl McDowell, and you must be the new hand."

"I'm Johnny Ragan! I'm pleased to meet you," drawled Johnny. Cheryl was fascinated by Johnny and his black curly hair. He'd filled out over the past week and was now a towering young giant. Of all the cowboys, this young man was nearer her age than the others. She blushed a deep red when she caught him looking at her. Johnny also blushed, and Erma saw the exchange between them.

"Come, Cheryl, Johnny needs some privacy, and I'm sure he's tired. Tom McDowell, as soon as he's talked with Red Hand, will be down to see you, Johnny. Rex sure gave you a good recommendation to Mr. McDowell. When you get rested up, I want to talk to you about the procedure Andy said you used in doctoring him," said Erma. "Supper will be at six. You may want to wash up and change your shirt. There's water in that pitcher and hot water in that teakettle. Come, Cheryl!"

Johnny took a sponge bath, washed his new shirt, and hung it on a line behind the large pot bellied stove to dry. He took off his long johns and washed them also. It was almost five o'clock before he could dress again. He was shaven and bathed and sitting in a chair when Andy woke.

"Golly, Johnny, is that you? What time is it? Five o'clock, and I still smell of the trail. The fellows will be in off the range anytime. Can I have this hot water?" he swept his hand toward the steaming teakettle.

"Cheryl was in to see you, along with Erma, and I tried to keep them back from you. They took one whiff and left here in a hurry," Johnny said with a smile. Andy groaned.

"Now that Erma is a looker and a lady! I don't care much about Cheryl, for she's still sort of young, but every cowboy on this ranch is crazy about Erma. Think if I washed my shirt it'd be dry by six? Man, is it hot in here! Guess you washed everything while I slept?" Andy groaned.

"I'll take those long johns and hang them on that line behind the bunkhouse while you take your sponge bath and hang your shirt on the line behind the stove," offered Johnny.

There was the sound of several horses entering the compound. Johnny looked out the window and saw about fifteen wranglers and cowboys riding toward one of the paddocks. They quickly pulled saddles, bridles, and blankets from their horses and put them over the top rail of the fence. Several had rags and began to rub down their horses before taking them to the water trough and giving them a drink. Several horses were turned out into the paddock, while others were taken into the barn.

One young cowboy was pulling a saddle and blanket from a horse. "Dad gum that William! When's he going to learn to take care of his own horse?" complained the wrangler.

"Never will, as long as you do it for him," stated another.

"Whose horse is that Grulla? There's Andy's horse too. They can't be back from Kansas yet," said another.

One cowboy rushed into the bunkhouse and stopped when he saw Johnny.

Andy had just finished his bath, yelled a "hello," and introduced Johnny. It wasn't long before Johnny had met them all. They were very busy washing and preparing for the evening meal. Word had spread quickly that Johnny had saved Andy's life and had stayed with him while he regained his strength, and Johnny was easily accepted into the family of the TM Ranch.

Someone clanged the triangular chime, and they all headed to supper at the summer kitchen. There were two long tables set for the meal. All found a place, and steaming hot foods were carried in by Erma and two black ladies.

A man Johnny estimated to be about forty clanged his glass, and everything got quiet. They all bowed their heads while Tom McDowell said the prayer for the food. Food was passed, and the black ladies and Erma stood to refill glasses with water and get additional food from the kitchen.

"We've a new member in our TM family, and it's good to see Andy back and recovering from an injury. I believe that you've all met Johnny Ragan by now. Johnny saved our cook from drowning when the herd was crossing the Canadian. In a scrimmage with a band of Indians, Andy was hit by an arrow, which penetrated his left lung. The arrow was extracted, and Andy nearly died. Had it not been for Johnny and an extraordinary procedure, Andy may have died. We all extend to Johnny our very highest gratitude and praise our God for sparing Andy."

The entire crew looked at Johnny, who was blushing a deep red and sat with his eyes looking into the glass he held. Andy stood and looked toward Johnny and led the applause. Johnny's blush deepened. The crew went back to eating, and Mr. McDowell walked to Johnny and said, "I want to speak to you when you've finished your meal. Take your time and eat, and then we'll talk."

Following the meal, Johnny and Andy approached their boss as he sat at the head of the table with a cup of coffee in his hand. Tom McDowell told them to sit down across the table from him so they could have eye contact.

Johnny shook hands with Tom McDowell, noting the rancher's penetrating eyes. They were kind eyes—not stern but observant. Tom took out the letter Rex had written and read it again silently while Johnny and Andy looked and waited.

"Rex tells me that you saved the chuck wagon from capsizing and thus saved our cook and his provisions. He also told in this letter that you killed a deer at four hundred yards with one shot. But to add to it all, you saved Andy here when Rex and Slim and the cook had given up on him and expected him to die." His eyes lifted from the letter and fixed on Johnny.

"I've seen more than one fellow soldier die from a gunshot through his lungs, and it isn't pleasant to see," said Tom McDowell. "We need to praise the good Lord for leading you to do what you did so Andy could breathe."

"Red Hand was following the herd and came upon us and wanted to see Johnny shoot his gun. Johnny killed a deer eight hundred yards away with one shot," said Andy. "I saw him do it."

Tom again turned his eyes on Johnny.

"What kind of gun do you have?" asked Tom.

"It's a sharps 1863 0.54 caliber rifle, sir, with double triggers."

"How old are you, young man?"

"I believe that I'm eighteen, sir. My dad was wounded horribly at Vicksburg. He came home, and his convalescence killed my mother. I was eleven."

"I want you to come on up to the house and meet my family," said Tom. "Andy, you know them well but come along too."

The three approached the hacienda from the front of the house. Johnny was all eyes, for the house was massive and beautiful. They entered through the kitchen and met Erma and the servants again as they were clearing the table in the dining room.

There was the sound of piano music, and a man with an excellent tenor voice was singing.

"In the sweet by and by, we shall meet on the beautiful shore, in the sweet by and by, we shall meet on the beautiful shore."

The music stopped. Tom led Johnny and Andy into the parlor. A young man sat on a chair reading, and Cheryl laid down her book to look at the newest employee, who was now cleaned of the trail dirt with a new shirt and a scarf at his throat. His black hair was wavy, and Johnny looked at her and smiled.

"Melody, Cheryl, William, and George, this is Johnny Ragan, our most recent employee and, may I add, our youngest. He saved Andy's life when Andy was hit by an arrow up in the Oklahoma Territory. He also saved the cook from drowning. Quite an accomplishment for such a young man! Of course you all know Andy," stated Tom McDowell.

Johnny approached the piano and bowed to Melody McDowell. "Pleased to meet you ma'am." He shook hands with George, but William did not move so he nodded toward him. Cheryl met him over halfway. "I met him when Erma went to see about Andy." Johnny took her hand in his and bowed, which caused her to smile. She usually did not pay much attention to boys, but there was something about this young man that drew her attention.

George was watching closely and said a few words to Johnny and to Andy.

"I'm feeling great now, but for a couple of weeks it was touch and go. If it weren't for Johnny, I know I wouldn't be here," added Andy.

"Do you sing?" asked Melody. Johnny noticed then what a very beautiful lady Mrs. McDowell was. Her light brown hair hung to the middle of her back. Her face was oval, and her large blue eyes were wide set. Her person was neat, and her smiling mouth was generous.

"I see where Cheryl gets a lot of her charm," said Johnny, and the saying pleased both Cheryl and her mother.

"Do you sing?" asked Melody.

"I sing to the cows at night! Every once in a while they bawl at me. I've never sung to a person, and I'm not sure what effect it might have," Johnny said, grinning.

"Know the new song we were singing?" asked George. "We sing a lot of religious songs. If you know it and want to sing along then let's try it."

"Yes, sir!" answered Johnny. Melody played a short introduction, and George led with his tenor voice.

"There's a land that is fairer than day…" Johnny began in his baritone voice to harmonize with George. "And by faith we can see it afar…"

Tom McDowell sat up, as did Cheryl, while Melody smiled and George grinned. "For the Father waits over the way, to prepare us a dwelling place there…" The song went on to conclusion and Melody led the applause.

"Great!" called Tom, and Andy cheered with Cheryl, whereas William smiled. Several other songs were sung, and soon Johnny felt completely at home. It had been so many years ago that his mother had taught him the words to the hymns and he had sung along with her.

"Welcome to the TM Ranch," said Tom. William merely nodded. Andy, George, and Johnny headed for the bunkhouse.

"Johnny," said George, "you're going to fit in well here. I hope you'll make this place your home and have many years here."

"I didn't seem to come off too well with William," said Johnny.

"Don't be concerned about that. He's that way to everyone. His dad lets him get by with more than he should," said George. "That's just between us." George left them for his bunk, and Andy grinned at Johnny.

"Cheryl made up a lot for her twin brother. I believe she showed more interest in you than she has in anybody else." Andy smiled. Johnny groaned.

"How old is she anyway?" asked Johnny.

"She is … let's see … just turned sixteen. She rides as well as her brother, and you can see her working among the horses with the best of them. She's a real tomboy. Erma has been watching her around the cowboys, as Cheryl doesn't seem to realize that she's a girl."

"Her mother sure is a beautiful woman and a very caring lady and mother," said Johnny. "Sure like our boss, too."

"Yes, she mothers us all, and we would all give our lives for her," said Andy. "Erma is well loved too. Tom was a real fighter when he bought this place but has mellowed a lot. He's a good Christian."

Johnny lay in his bed for some time, thanking God for the new home and the love that he had seen in his new family. Everything had quieted down, and Johnny went off to sleep.

JOHNNY GETS A RAISE
AND A NEW WINCHESTER

Johnny was taken north and rode with Amos, who was the head scout of the ranch.

"I want you to pay a lot of attention to Amos. He's savvy in the scouting business," said George. "We have three line shacks on the northern edge of the ranch, where various cowboys stay. We've been losing a few cows to rustlers, which is something new for us. Slim Wilkins has a reputation of being very quick with a gun and has kept the rustling to a minimum. They seem to know when he isn't around and make small strikes when he's away. We're moving Amos up there, as we lost fifty head last week to rustlers. Watch and you'll learn a lot from Amos."

Amos was about fifty-seven and had homesteaded land adjoining the TM Ranch. He was married to Red Hand's sister and had constructed a home on his homesteaded property. Wolf Fang, her father, spent a lot of time with his daughter, and Amos and Wolf Fang were close friends. The old Indian often rode with Amos on scouting trips. Red Hand was the acting chief of the tribe but often came to Wolf Fang for advice.

Amos had an Indian scout that worked closely with him. Eagle Feather was considered the best tracker in the panhandle of Texas. He was a cousin to Amos's wife and had been hired when Matt Willard, a former Texas Ranger, was security boss at the ranch. Eagle Feather had lived in a wigwam on Matt's thousand-acre ranch, near the top of the Cap Rock on the western part of the property.

Matt and Bess Willard were the parents of Tom McDowell's first wife, Delight, and Melody and Tom looked up to them as if they were their parents. Cheryl often rode over to see Grandmother and Grandfather, and they spoiled the girl with their extravagant love. William spent more time with Matt and Bess than he did at the TM Ranch. Matt and Bess often had the McDowell's two younger children, Howard and Katherine, at their ranch.

Johnny Ragan met Matt Willard at the line shack the third night he was there. Amos, Eagle Feather, and Johnny had been scouting along the Cap Rock and above it for signs of the missing fifty cattle. Eagle Feather had showed Amos some signs, and the faint trail led off to the west.

Amos asked Johnny if he would go back to the line camp and get a couple pack mules with enough provisions for a week for the three of them. Johnny did so and carefully planned what he would need to take with him.

He was in the process when Matt rode to the front of the house and William was with him. Matt did not know Johnny and held his hand near his six gun while he questioned him. William walked to the line shack from the corral and introduced Matt to Johnny.

"Thought I had gotten me one of those rustlers stealing supplies," drawled Matt. "I guess once a Ranger, always a Ranger. Now, son, you should never let yourself get caught that unprepared. Suppose that I had been a rustler. I would have had the draw on you."

"I saw William and knew him, and just in case, I have my six-shooter in my right hand under this sack of flour." Johnny smiled.

"Well I'll be. You had me covered all the time. I'm Matt Willard."

"I'm Johnny Ragan, sir. I've heard of you from Amos," said Johnny.

"Where are Amos and Eagle Feather?" asked William.

"We've been up on the Cap Rock and Eagle Feather found some old sign of those fifty steers that were rustled or missing, and they sent me back for some supplies that we'll need while trailing them. Amos said the tracks were headed into New Mexico. As late as it is, I decided to wait till early morning, as this is the first time that I've been in this area," said Johnny.

"If I was twenty years younger, I'd go along." Matt smiled. William showed no interest in the least. The three of them bedded down for the night at the Line Camp, and Matt was up fixing breakfast when William came down from the loft.

"Where's Johnny?" asked Matt.

"I have no idea," answered William.

"Foods to be packed are lying there in the corner, so he must be around here somewhere." William stood looking toward the stable.

"He's out there watering the mules and his Grulla," he said. William was a little put out that Johnny had gotten a head start on them, for William was still headstrong and would pout over anything that displeased him.

Johnny came in, and Matt told him that the bacon was ready and asked how many eggs he wanted.

"Give me four over lightly, please. Hi, Matt and William. It's beginning to get pink in the east, and what a beautiful day is dawning," drawled Johnny.

Matt had fried a dozen eggs and made biscuits. Matt bowed his head, gave thanks for the food, and made a prayer that all would be safe for the day. William and Johnny both said, "Amen."

The three of them ate in silence until Matt asked Johnny, "How old are you, son?"

"Reckon I'm about eighteen," answered Johnny.

"I'm sixteen," said William. Johnny nodded to William.

"Where you from?" asked Matt.

"Just north of San Antonio," Johnny answered and continued eating.

"Got any parents, son?" asked Matt.

"No, sir, Dad was wounded at Vicksburg and came home to die, and it killed my ma. I was eleven then, and I've been lonely ever since. Sure like it here and hope that Mr. McDowell will keep me on."

"Don't see why he shouldn't," said Matt. The breakfast was finished, and Matt said he would wash the dishes so Johnny could get a good start. Johnny thanked him and loaded the supplies on the two pack mules. Matt watched and checked things in his mind while William stood by, not eager to help with any of the chores.

"Here, take this compass just in case you get turned around out there. That arrow will always point north."

Johnny took notice and thanked him then pulled out just as the sun began to peep over the valley.

"A fine young man," said Matt. William didn't answer but was considering what Matt was saying. "He's all right, I guess, but he'll never have anything and will always be a drover," said William.

"Some things are more valuable than gold, William," said Matt.

"What?"

"A good name is more valuable than gold," quoted Matt from his Bible. William thought on it for a while. "Aw, Granddad, I would rather have the gold than a good name."

"I knew a friend who discovered gold and died with it in his pockets. He died of thirst, for he had run out of water. What do you think he thought more valuable?"

"I guess water," said William.

"Right!" agreed Matt. Someone needed to teach William just where true values lie, and Matt planned to get the job done.

Johnny was climbing the cap rock to the west and headed into New Mexico. This was Indian country, and he was very alert. He took the oil cloth off his Sharp rifle and checked it to see if it was loaded. In the distance he could see the outlines of a mountain range, and he began to hum the song George and he had sung together. "There's a land that is fairer than day and by faith we can see it afar ... For the Father waits over the way ... " Johnny stopped his horse when he heard shooting in the far distance.

"Caught up with them, and I'm too far away to give them help. I shouldn't have stayed at the line camp." He put the horses into a cantor and turned toward the distant shooting. He rode all morning, and the gun battle appeared to be close. Johnny took his Sharp and hobbled his horse and mules. He climbed a hill and crawled to the edge of the battlefield. Eagle Feather and Amos were pinned down by half a dozen rustlers. Three men lay inert, and it appeared Amos and Eagle Feather had inflicted some damage. The cattle could be seen in a flat near a water hole, and it was plain they would not leave the water.

Johnny took from his oil cloth a metal rod that he used as a brace when he fired his gun at great distances. He rested the Sharp on the rod and checked the shell and cap. He estimated the distance at a thousand yards and raised the rear sight and peep sight. He could see that the rustlers had the high ground, but his position was slightly above theirs. One of the rustlers was standing out of sight of Amos and leaning against a rock.

Johnny had never shot at a human being before. He sighted at the distant rustler and pulled the first trigger. He sighted again and squeezed. The huge gun fired, and the recoil was fierce. He reached for a second shell and firing cap. He heard the spat of the bullet hitting flesh and saw the man fall backward into the rocks. Amos and Eagle Feather were trying to locate him. The two rustlers were trying to find better cover. He watched one of the rustlers crawling toward better cover on his belly.

He aimed carefully, and again the huge gun recoiled. The man was struck on the side of his head, which exploded into flesh, blood, and shattered bone. The last rustler stood and threw his gun away, and Amos turned and waved to the unknown shooter that he could not see. The rustler stood with his arms straight up and tried to find the shooter.

Eagle Feather was first to see Johnny as he mounted his Grulla and led the mules on down to the trail. "Wow, him a good shot." Eagle Feather smiled.

"Hello, Johnny, I'm impressed!" said Amos. "You sure saved our bacon! We were low on shells and water. We figured you would stay at the house last night, so we weren't looking for you for another hour. What in the world are you shooting? You were lying on that hilltop, weren't you? I thought that I saw the smoke from the gun once when you fired!"

While Eagle Feather held his gun on the rustler and searched him, Johnny handed Amos the Sharp.

"This is an 1863 model, isn't it? I heard they were great on Buffalo and can see why now." He looked at the two men Johnny had shot and estimated the distance from where he had fired to be a thousand yards.

"Amazing! Wait 'til I tell the boss! Johnny, you can be my scout, and Eagle Feather will be happy to have you as our partner. You sure saved our lives," said Amos. The rustler was tied to his horse, and Amos, Johnny, and Eagle Feather started the herd back toward the TM Ranch. The rustlers were buried under rocks at the side of the trail. They left no marker, for rustling was a capital offense in those days. Usually they were hung, but there had been enough killing, and the remaining rustler was thankful the big gun had not been aimed at him.

Johnny rode along silently. He had killed two men, and the thought of it kept him quiet. Matt and William were still at the line camp, and Matt took charge of the rustler while Amos, Johnny, and Eagle Feather put the cattle back into a paddock, where they had water and feed.

Matt sat and listened to Amos and Eagle Feather tell of Johnny's rescue and of the shooting of the two rustlers. Johnny left when they began talking and went out to see about his horse and the two mules.

"Wonder if those two were the first that he killed?" asked Matt.

"The first two would be the most difficult, you know," said Amos. "I owe my life to him, and so does Eagle Feather."

William asked Amos to tell him what Johnny had done, and when Amos finished he went to Eagle Feather and asked him his version. He found in young Johnny a hero, and his devotion for Johnny began right then and there. He left the room to help Johnny with the horses.

Matt thought that Johnny would be a great influence on William. William's education began that afternoon and continued for a week. Johnny took him down behind the dwelling, along the river, and watched him while he shot Matt's Winchester. William was pulling the trigger instead of squeezing it; William needed to hold his breath just prior to squeezing the trigger. Johnny taught him how to adjust for the wind, and with Johnny's critical eye William greatly improved his shooting.

Upon his return to the ranch, Tom McDowell called Johnny into his office.

Amos and Eager Feather had made their reports, and Tom knew that the cattle had been returned.

"Next week I'm raising Johnny's pay to sixty dollars a month and presenting him with a new Winchester. I feel from your report that he's earned it. I need to see him shoot, though. Let him earn the money and the Winchester as all the cowboys have done."

"Boss, I would like to see him shoot too," said Amos. "I believe you will be amazed as I was." Right after breakfast, as the cowboys began to make preparations for branding cattle, and Johnny and William were finishing breakfast Tom came to the kitchen door and called Johnny to one side.

"Get your Sharp rifle and come with me," said Tom. William followed Johnny while he collected his rifle, shells, and caps. There was a rifle range about half a mile from the hacienda, where many of the cowboys practiced their shooting and where William and Johnny had been doing the same.

"Amos said that you were a good shot, and I want you to prove it to me. Let me see if you can hit that target."

"Which one, sir? That one or that one." Johnny pointed to one on a tree at one hundred yards and one at eight hundred yards.

"Try them both," said Tom. Amos stood back, smiling.

Johnny put the shell into the breech, placed the cap, lifted the gun, and quickly squeezed the first trigger then the second. The big gun roared!

William ran and brought back the target.

"Dead center, Dad!" called the boy. Tom looked the target over and said,

"Try the other one." Johnny loaded the breach with a shell and placed the cap. He pulled the first trigger and squeezed the second trigger. The big gun roared. William rushed out to retrieve the second target.

"Dead center, Dad!" called William and brought the target to Tom. Amos stood behind Tom and grinned.

"Good shooting, Johnny. Today you'll get your pay raised, and here's your new Winchester." He handed a box to Johnny and William stood by as Johnny unwrapped a Winchester 1873 model. Tom loaded the Winchester and handed it to Johnny.

"Try the target at one hundred yards."

Johnny lifted it to his cheek a couple times then shot with rapid fire toward the tree. William retrieved the target, and there were ten shots dead center in the target. Tom smiled his satisfaction and turned and started for the bunkhouse.

"Sir, wait a minute! William, replace that target for me!" asked Johnny. William complied. Upon his return, Johnny handed the gun to William and said, "You try." Tom stood, amazed, as his son shot eight out of ten holes into the middle of the target.

"Well, I'll be! Son, you get a new Winchester too, and your salary is $60.00 a month. I'm proud of you! You've earned it." A tear came to his eyes and he looked at Johnny and whispered, "Thank you."

To have achieved what was the aim of all the cowboys really lifted William's spirit, and from that time on William became an extra good cowboy and learned the ranching business. The boy was filling out and would soon be as big as his dad. He invaded his dad's office and studied the books and the profit and loss sheets. His dad explained some of the ways that he kept his books, and William made suggestions from his courses in economics that Tom saw as improvements to his bookkeeping.

"My husband, our son, has grown up, and I like him as well as love him. It was hard to like him there for a while, but he's a dear now. What changed him?"

"That Johnny had a great influence on him, and now William is helping Johnny," said Tom. "When our tutor comes to teach William and Cheryl, I'm going to ask Johnny if he would like to take schooling too. The extra cost won't be much, and I appreciate Johnny for what he has done with William."

"My husband, have you noticed how Cheryl has been taking notice of Johnny? Is Johnny the kind of person that Cheryl will fall in love with?"

"Honey, she's just a child!"

"She's the same age as William, and you have him earning a man's income. You're teaching William to shoot, ride, and brand cattle. You think of him as a man and Cheryl as a child? The looks that she's been giving Johnny are the looks of a mature woman in love."

Tom was shocked and sat down to think about the situation. Cheryl must go to college as well as William. *Am I pressing William too hard? Maybe I need to move Johnny away from William and definitely from Cheryl—for a while anyway. I'll send Johnny to the Kiowa tribe and see what the missionary work will do in his life.*

Tom McDowell immediately took pen, ink, and paper and sat at his desk and wrote a letter to John Beasley. This was the minister who baptized Melody, Bess, Matt, as well as George, Erma, and Rex.

"Amos, I want you to take Johnny to Red Hand's Kiowa tribe and stay with him for a couple of weeks while Johnny gets acquainted with John Beasley.

●

"Johnny, Cheryl wants to see you!" said William the next day.

"Dad had a long talk with me this morning about sending Cheryl and me back to Virginia to school. He was seventeen when he attended Virginia Military Institute in Lexington, Virginia, and wants me to attend school there also. I was especially interested in Engineering, but since we've become such good friends, I'm more interested in ranching. Cheryl has become very interested in you, as you may or may not know, and you're the only boy that she has ever noticed. Dad wants her to go to a girl's finishing school."

"Your dad doesn't approve of me?" asked Johnny in a strange voice. He had always thought Tom McDowell thought highly of him.

"It isn't you, Johnny. Dad thinks the sun rises and sets on Cheryl and wants her to be one of those eastern educated ladies. He wants her to be the wife of some big executive, I guess. But I know she loves you, Johnny."

"Loves me? William, I'm nothing. I own nothing. I have a brother and a sister but haven't seen them in seven years. I'm not even sure they are alive! I have this horse that is getting pretty old. I have the clothes that are on my back, a Sharp rifle, a Winchester, and sixty dollars, which is my first month's pay. Why does Cheryl love me? I've never been in love, and have no idea what it would be like to be in that condition," said Johnny.

"I feel just awful!" said Johnny. "Your dad is angry at me because Cheryl feels that way toward me, and I've nothing to do with it. Let's go see Cheryl."

William and Johnny rode around the side of the hill behind the hacienda and approached a small wooded area near the top of the hill. Cheryl was sitting on a rock and had the reins of her horse in her hand. Johnny was shocked when he saw her in a riding habit, instead of her usual corduroy pants. Her hair was piled on her head, and her eyes were red. She had on a light blue blouse, which highlighted the enormous blue of her eyes.

William said, "Hi, sis! I brought him like I promised." He clucked to his horse and rode away.

Johnny slowly dismounted and approached Cheryl.

"Cheryl, you wanted to see me? You sure look nice!" said Johnny.

"Oh, Johnny! William and I are being sent far off to Virginia to school. William will be going to Virginia Military Institute, and I will be attending Hollins University in Roanoke, Virginia. Will you write to me? I'll write to you! Johnny, I can't help it, but I love you so! Mother saw me watching you, and she told Dad, and now he's sending me away, and William too. I believe he's sending you to the Kiowa tribe to separate us, I guess."

She moved slightly toward him, and he rushed to meet her. They embraced in an awkward way at first, but then their lips found each other, and he kissed her fiercely.

"It was just like I thought it would be!" whispered Cheryl.

"Your dad would kill me if he knew," groaned Johnny. "I'll send my love each time that I write to you. Johnny, how my heart aches." She turned and kissed Johnny one more time and then was on her horse and racing for the house.

He sat with his face in his hands on the rock where she had sat. William was there and sat on his horse while Johnny regained some of his composure.

"We leave tomorrow, so I must get back to the house and pack," said William.

Johnny and William retraced their steps back down the hill away from the hacienda and rode to the bunkhouse.

Later, Amos came into the room and approached William and Johnny. "I hate to break this up, but William, you need to pack, and Johnny, you and I will be leaving here in half an hour. The boss wants you to spend some time with the Kiowa."

William was sad when he said good-bye to his pard Johnny. Johnny thought that day to be the saddest of his young life. He rode up the valley following Amos and turned to wave at Cheryl, William, Melody, and Tom McDowell as they all stood in the front yard of the hacienda and waved farewell.

JOHNNY AT THE KIOWA CAMP

Johnny and Amos rode into the grasslands of Oklahoma, and Amos thought it a good time to talk with Johnny. His eyesight was not as sharp as it was when he scouted for Fremont back in New Mexico, but his ears were still picking up the sounds of nature. In the past twenty years he had fathered three children with his wife, Red Doe, who was the daughter to Wolf Fang and Little Doe and sister to Red Hand, chief of the Kiowa. He had homesteaded one hundred sixty acres, and his cowboy friends had helped him build a home there, adjacent to the TM Ranch and Matt's MBD Ranch.

"Johnny, Tom, and Melody are great people and have done a lot of good things for many people. Red Doe and I owe them so much, for they provide us a good living. They have befriended Wolf Fang and his tribe, of which Red Hand is now chief. You know what they're doing is not against you but to educate and protect their children. When their two youngest children become of college age, they'll do the same for them. Don't feel harshly against Tom and Melody," said Amos.

Johnny took what was said by Amos and thought on it awhile.

"You know, Amos, I've come to love that William like a brother. I have a brother somewhere that I haven't seen in seven years. William has changed completely, into a very likeable young man, and I feel that some of the credit belongs to me. I trained him to shoot and to become responsible both to those around him and to God. I'm amazed that Cheryl shows such affection to an hombre like me, for I do not deserve it."

Amos didn't answer, and they both rode on in silence until they saw in the distance the Kiowa village, and Amos felt he should tell Johnny more about the tribe before they arrived.

"Tom McDowell made friends with Wolf Fang in 1866 when he first bought the ranchero from a Spaniard. Wolf Fang and Tom traded amongst themselves and became friends, and Red Hand is very friendly with Tom. They hunted together and still do. Back in 1867, a year after Tom bought the ranch, the Kiowa, Cheyenne, Comanche, and Arapaho—in a treaty known as the Medicine Lodge Treaty—joined together and agreed to go onto a reservation. Custer's slaughter of women and children at Washita in 1868 hurried the fulfillment of the treaty. Some troubles between the Indian tribes and the military ended with Lone Wolf and many of his followers being deported to Florida for three years. John Beasley, a Christian missionary who did such a great work at our ranch, was introduced to Wolf Fang and managed to win many of the Indians to Jesus Christ. John Beasley married a daughter to Wolf Fang, Causes to Laugh, and together they're still working among the tribe. Wolf Fang and Red Hand were led to Christ and brought this local tribe to the reservation. Other tribes resisted the military and Setangya, one of the main chiefs, was shot and killed while resisting arrest. Settainti, another main chief, committed suicide in prison. So the peaceful method, followed by Red Hand, was the true way to go and Red Hand gave the credit to his Lord Jesus Christ. He credits John Beasley for telling him of Christ and when Lone Wolf, another chief, led a group of hostile Kiowa in an uprising, Red Hand refused to join them, and the tribe was saved from reprisal and possible destruction.

"There is a Quaker teacher that is working in our tribe too. His name is Thomas C. Battery, and he's done much to instruct our people in reading, writing, and arithmetic. John Beasley, however, is our main teacher, and Causes to Laugh speaks English well and is one of the main causes for the ministry of John. They've been married seventeen years and have two children, Ruth and Ben. Ruth is sixteen, I believe, and Ben is fourteen," continued Amos.

Approximately a hundred and fifty wigwams surrounded a half-dozen frame dwellings, and a United Sates flag hung over one of the larger buildings. The buildings were adobe and all one level, but the larger was a two-story adobe with double hung windows. A porch was across the front, with a balcony over the porch. This was the commissioner's building, trading station, and U.S. Post Office.

Amos rode by the trading post as Johnny took notice of several Indians who stood on the porch and stared at their visitors. Some were attired in white men's clothing and had older, brightly colored shirts and corduroy trousers. The colors were faded, and the men were gaunt, their clothing was dirty. The men had headbands with a single feather. Their hair was mostly braided, but a couple had cowboy hats, and their dark hair was tucked under the brim.

"Not what I expected to find!" said Johnny to Amos.

"Things have really changed, and I'm not so sure that it's for the better," answered Amos. "Those men are there until they are given food, and it appears that is their ambition in life. The old life would have them out on the plains, seeking to bring home their kill to their families."

Amos stopped at a large tepee near the center of the camp, where Red Hand was standing in the doorway. He called to Amos in the Kiowa tongue, and Amos saluted him in return. Amos hugged Red Hand and turned to introduce Johnny.

"Welcome to our camp, Johnny," said Red Hand. "Come into our tepee. Our home is your home."

Red Hand led them into the interior of the tepee, where he motioned them to sit on soft buffalo robes. Amos handed Red Hand the letter from Tom McDowell.

A very pretty Indian girl entered and stood smiling at Amos.

"This is the wife of Red Hand, and her name is White Swan," introduced Amos. "This is Johnny Ragan."

She was dressed in deerskin, and her form was lean and straight. Her eyes were brown, and her black hair was braided. She had a pug nose, her mouth was generous, and she was radiant in smile and personality.

"How do you do?" she asked Johnny in excellent English and offered a small hand to him. Johnny bowed, took her hand, and returned her smile.

"I'm fine and you?"

She nodded. "Fine, thank you! Have you met Causes to Laugh? She is more than a sister-in-law to me. She and her husband are the very best Christians in our tribe."

"Johnny is a great hunter," Red Hand said, "a healer, and will be with us for a while. He will be staying at the mission, for Tom McDowell wants him to be taught by Tom Battery and John Beasley, according to his letter. I will discuss this with the two of them. Wait here, and I will be back soon." Red hand left the tepee on his errand.

"Please be seated!" said White Swan. "How is my brother?" She looked to Amos for reply.

"Eagle Feather sends his love to his little sister," answered Amos. Johnny sat up straight, for Eagle Feather was the scout who worked with Amos and was scouting for the TM Ranch.

"Eagle Feather is a cousin of yours?" he asked Amos.

Amos answered by nodding yes.

"Eagle Feather is an excellent scout."

Red Hand had returned and was entering the door when Amos began to tell White Swan how Johnny had rescued Eagle Feather and him. Red Hand immediately turned his attention to Amos.

"We could hear the bullet strike the rustlers before we heard Johnny's gun. The rustlers couldn't see him but could see the effect of his shot. Both Eagle Feather and I owe our lives to Johnny."

White Swan turned toward Johnny. "Thank you for saving my beloved brother and my cousin Amos."

"This only adds to your fame as being a great shot. We appreciate what you have done for us," said Red Hand. "Causes to Laugh and John Beasley are waiting for you at the Mission and look forward to your being with them for several moons. You are a guest of our tribe for what you have done!" he added.

Amos and Johnny bid Red Hand and White Swan good-bye, and Amos and Johnny led their horses to the Mission building, where John Beasley and Causes to Laugh were waiting on the front porch.

John was a slight man with red hair and a red beard. He wore a blue jacket and a light blue plain shirt with brown corduroy trousers. This was his usual working outfit, as he taught in various classes throughout the day.

"The good Lord has sent us a helpmate," said John and shook Johnny's hand.

"This is my wife, Causes to Laugh." Causes to Laugh was dressed in deer skins, but there was a small jacket that was buttoned at her breast. Johnny was amazed by her beauty. Her black hair was braided, and her brown eyes were beautiful and full of love, concern, and happiness. Johnny estimated her age to be in her late thirties. She had an excellent figure and moved gracefully.

"I am happy to know you, Johnny. We have a letter from Tom McDowell and hope that you can learn here and be of a benefit to the Mission also."

There was movement in the Mission door, and a young lady who was the spitting image of Causes to Laugh smiled a greeting to Amos and then turned her brown eyes on Johnny. Her hair was auburn and was braided like her mother's. She was very mature in body and charm for her age, and Johnny was captivated by her the moment he saw her.

"This is our daughter, Ruth, and here comes Ben," said John Beasley. The boy also had red hair but was big for his age—awkward—and estimated to be about twelve. He was dressed in leggings and had a single feather in his hair.

"Glad to meet you both," said Johnny, but most of his attention was on Ruth.

"We have a corral at the rear of the Mission, so why don't you take your horse around there? Ruth will show you where to put him. Do you have a war bag? Luggage?" asked John.

"No, sir, I need to buy a change of clothes at the trading post, if I can," answered Johnny. He had a hundred dollars in his pocket. That was more money than he had ever had, and he was proud of his good fortune.

Ruth led him to the corral behind the mission. She attempted to take the bridle off the Grulla, but the horse shied away from her.

"Don't feel bad, for she is a one-person horse. She's always been mine, and no one else can ride her or care for her. My uncle tried to steal her from me, and she bucked him off. That was seven years ago, and no one else has ever tried to ride her since."

Ruth stood near Johnny's Grulla and patted her and talked to her. The horse rolled her eyes at Ruth and laid her ears back. Ruth saw this and moved back.

"I see what you mean! I usually can tame most wild horses, but this one will be a challenge. I hope that I might have the time to try to win her affection." Ruth pointed to a manger adjacent to the corral.

"There's an empty stall in there, where you can keep her. Hay and oats are in the loft above the stall. Let's hurry, for the Mission will be serving dinner in a few minutes. Mom will want you to know where you'll be staying." She turned and smiled at Johnny, and he blushed a crimson red.

Causes to Laugh took Johnny under her wing and showed the young man where he would be staying. She made his bed for him and carried water from the big well so he could wash and prepare himself for the meal.

Johnny shaved away his growing beard and took his old comb and parted his hair on the side. His thoughts went back to the TM ranch and to Andy and the other cowboys who must be doing the same thing about now. If they ever saw Ruth, there would be a bunch of very lovesick cowboys. What would Cheryl think? With this thought in his mind, he walked from his room into the Mission dining room, which was half full of Indian children and a half-dozen adults.

John Beasley, dressed in a black suit, offered prayer for the food and all cried, "Amen!" The children jabbered in their native tongue while the adults tried to get them to speak English. He knew that he was the subject of the conversations of many of the diners and was self-conscious as he sat next to John Beasley and Causes to Laugh and across from Ruth and Ben.

"Sir," Johnny said to John Beasley, "you have an excellent family, and I can see that you all love the good Lord."

"You couldn't have said anything that pleases me more than to hear such words from you!" said John. "I presume, then, that you are a Christian?"

"I have blood on my hands, sir! I have read the Bible and know much of its teachings, but I need to know more relative to salvation. I have killed two men and have been very ashamed since it happened," said Johnny.

"Did you murder them?" asked John.

"I have not thought of that. I shot them because they were shooting at my friends, Amos and Eagle Feather. The men had rustled TM cattle," added Johnny. "But I shot them as I would shoot at a distant tree, and this terrible feeling that I had killed them came when I was near enough to them to see they were men and not trees. Will God forgive me for killing people that He made in His own image? The job that I have may call for me to kill others, to protect TM Cowboys or the members of that family. Can I be a Christian and do that?"

John Beasley sat with his head down, thought for a while, and said, "It needs a lot of thought, and we will study the scriptures in class, and just maybe the scriptures will give us an answer. I don't think that you committed murder but administered justice under the authority of the laws of our land. You served as a magistrate administering justice, and you weren't carrying the sword in vain," said John Beasley. "The subject needs a lot more thought, and we'll wrestle with this in class, just you and me. God will forgive every sin that we have committed, except the sin against the Holy Ghost."

Johnny continued to eat but toyed some with his food. Ruth had heard most of the discussion that Johnny had with her dad and turned sad eyes toward her new friend.

With the dinner completed, John Beasley began to sing, "Praise God from whom all blessings flow ... " Everyone joined in to sing unto the father for the food that God had given them. Johnny joined in with them, and Causes to Laugh and John Beasley looked in wonder as Johnny's deep baritone voice rose in volume, "Praise, Father, Son and Holy Ghost. Amen!"

"God has sent us someone to lead us in our singing," said Causes to Laugh, and John Beasley agreed. Ruth sat and looked in amazement at Johnny, for the Kiowa sang in guttural language, and not the baritone that she had heard from Johnny's mouth.

Johnny decided to explore the trading post and post office. There he met Superintendent William Schmitt. He had been appointed to office by General Phil Sheridan, a northern general who was in charge of reconstruction in the area and had been there since the Indians were put on the reservation. Superintendent Schmitt was slight of build and slightly bald.

He wore wire glasses and dressed in a faded shirt and corduroy trousers with suspenders. When he saw Johnny, he came to him and introduced himself. Johnny said he would be receiving mail there and planned to be at the Mission for some time. Johnny bought another shirt and two pair of trousers as well as handkerchiefs and a pair of moccasins.

"Let's see! That will be $3.95. Do you have that much, young man?" asked Mr. Schmitt.

Johnny hid his money as he found four dollars and saw the wonder come to Mr. Schmitt's face. He took the nickel change and concealed his money in a large handkerchief.

"We have billfolds, if you want to buy one? They're twenty-five cents and are made of deer skins," added Superintendent Schmitt.

Johnny found another dollar, and this time Mr. Schmitt managed to see several twenty-dollar bills in Johnny's possession. Johnny turned his back to put all his cash in his new billfold. He got his seventy-five cents change and walked out of the trading post toward the Mission House.

Mr. Schmitt motioned with his finger, and two Apache Indians hurried to him. He whispered to them, and they followed Johnny into the night.

Johnny had tried on the moccasins and liked their feel so well that he was carrying his heavy boots that were hobnailed. He turned to see someone exit from the trading post and was aware of someone following him. Johnny was a good six-feet-four inches tall and weighed two hundred ten pounds. Without his heavy boots, he was very light on his feet.

A shadow flashed toward him, and he saw the gleam of a knife. He swung a heavy boot into the attacker's face, and the hobnailed heel caught the attacker flush on the forehead. The attacker fell with a dull thud as the second attacker rushed by. Johnny felt the sharp pain of the knife as it tore his clothes and cut into his arm. With his right arm he circled the attacker's neck, thrust his right leg into the small of the man's back, and yanked backwards. The man's feet went over his head, and there was a groan and a thud as the man struck the hard ground. Johnny saw the glint of the knife lying in the dirt, retrieved it, and then sat down on the struggling attacker.

"Amos!" called Johnny, and Amos and Red Hand were there in moments. Red Hand gave orders to others, and the two attackers were tied and carried to Red Hand's tepee.

"You hurt?" inquired Amos.

"I got cut on the arm," answered Johnny. "I don't know why they were attacking me."

"You flash any money in the trading post?" asked Amos. "Let's go to the Mission, and we'll see how badly you're hurt."

Causes to Laugh and Ruth were genuinely concerned when Amos and Johnny came into the Mission. Johnny's arm was bloodied, and his shirt that the cook had given him was torn.

"Take off that shirt and let's see!" said Amos. Johnny removed his shirt and undershirt, and there was a cut along his left bicep.

"It isn't bad, but it will be sore for a week," said Amos. Causes to Laugh took some solution and applied some salve and then bound it up in a clean cloth. Ruth stood staring at this very muscular young giant, until her mother saw Ruth's stare.

"Ruth, we don't need you now!" Ruth knew what she meant and quickly vanished to the dining hall of the Mission.

Red Hand came into the room and thanked Johnny for apprehending the two robbers.

"We've been having visitors robbed and murdered here at the reservation, and we believe you've caught the guilty party. The two are Kiowa Apache and not of my tribe. We'll contact Mr. Schmitt so that the Federal Soldiers can handle this. Johnny, you might need to appear at their trial. How badly were you knifed?"

"It isn't too bad!" said Amos. "He'll be sore for a few days."

"The attackers will both live, but it'll be a week before one will be able to see. What did you hit him with, Johnny?"

"Got him as he was coming in with my hobnailed heavy boot." Johnny smiled.

"The other one can't turn over and says his back may be broken," said Red Hand.

"A trick I picked up fighting near the railroad tracks with the Irish," answered Johnny. Johnny had his clothes back on, and he thanked Causes to Laugh. She gathered her medical supplies and was putting them away when she went to her husband and told John Beasley about the look that she had seen on Ruth's face.

"We must watch Ruth and try to arrange for her to have a husband. My husband, shall we let her select her own husband according to the way white people do, or shall we let the young men of my tribe bring their horses and woo her?"

John Beasley was taken aback. He looked at Causes to Laugh in amazement. "Our Ruth ready to marry?"

"She's eighteen!" said Causes to Laugh. John groaned.

"Did Johnny see her looking at him?" asked John.

"No! But I wonder what he thought when I sent her away," declared Causes to Laugh.

"My dear, when we married, I would have given a hundred horses for you, but I had none to give. I wanted and needed you, but was I ever thrilled when you told me that you loved me and would marry a poor preacher like me." John smiled.

"I love you more each day and feel that I am the most fortunate man in the world. What would I do without you?"

"I agree. Let's allow Ruth to select her own husband! Johnny is a fine young man, but I'll not be a matchmaker," said Causes to Laugh. "I wonder if he has a secret girlfriend?"

Johnny was sore for a few days but recovered well. Red Hand called him before the elders of the tribe, and the two attackers were sent to council before the Kiowa Apache for their punishment. Both of the attackers were Kiowa Apache, and they needed justice from their tribe.

The second week that Johnny was at the Mission, he received a letter from Cheryl. It came in a perfumed, blue envelope. Johnny stared at the letter and smiled as he thought of the girl and their rendezvous on the hill behind the hacienda. With shaking hands he tore open the letter. The letter was full of her trip by train into Roanoke, Virginia, and of the beauty of the Blue Ridge Mountains. She liked the school very much and was settling down to her studies.

"I miss you already, Johnny! Four years away is a very long time, but I'm considering it a test period for the both of us. If you find someone that you love more than me then feel free of any obligation to me. The same should be true with me, but this is a girl's school and I see only old professors. Don't worry, my love is genuine. Love, Cheryl."

Johnny read and reread the letter and returned again to "someone more than me." His thoughts went to Ruth. He must stay away from Ruth to really be true to Cheryl.

Johnny led the singing at the Missions and added what he could to help with the services. He took several courses, and John Beasley and Thomas C. Battery proved to be good teachers. In the evenings he would take his gun and hunt along the Cimarron River. Several Indians also hunted that area, but he shot the game at such distances that he killed much more than others and thus kept the Mission in fresh meat.

Fall slipped into winter, and the grasslands were cruel in that there was no refuge from the wintry winds that crossed the plains. Many of the trees along the Cimarron were cut down, and buffalo chips became more difficult to find. The Trading Post introduced kerosene stoves to help with fuel for the various lodges. Several of the Indians were nearly asphyxiated, for they did not understand about the uses of the stove pipe. John and Thomas Battery had classes and demonstrations to teach proper ventilation. Several gallons of kerosene were kept at the trading post to prevent the Indians from freezing during that winter.

Cheryl wrote every day, and Johnny looked forward to his trip to the post office. One day Ruth just happened to be in the post office when Johnny asked for his mail. He dropped the letter, and it fell to the floor at her feet. She picked it up, smelled it, and handed it to Johnny with a grin. He blushed.

"A special friend, Johnny?" she chided him.

"It is from Cheryl, daughter of Tom McDowell," stated Johnny truthfully.

"Oh, I know her. Mom use to take us to the hacienda to play with Cheryl and William. But that was many years ago, and we haven't seen them since Mother and Dad got so involved with the Mission. Have you been avoiding me, Johnny?" she asked seriously. "Is the reason tied up with Cheryl?"

"I thought you've been avoiding me! I used to see you out riding by yourself, but have you stopped because of the weather?" asked Johnny. "Cheryl and I write to each other, and I also write to William," he added.

"I still am able to ride when I want to. You want to go riding, Johnny? I'll need to okay it with Dad, for he has suddenly become very protective since those two tried to rob you. How about taking me hunting with you down by the Cimarron?"

"I'm going this afternoon and plan to be back for supper," invited Johnny then thought of his letter and turned away from Ruth to open and read the letter from Cheryl.

•

"I have a lot of confidence in Johnny, and Ruth, so I gave my permission for Johnny to take Ruth hunting with him this afternoon," John told Causes to Laugh. She nodded her agreement.

Ruth was an excellent rider, and her horse was of good stock. Johnny's Grulla was getting older and could not run long spells without getting winded. Johnny, therefore, humored her and let Ruth take the lead. Seeing she could not provoke a race, Ruth pulled up and waited for Johnny. The two rode side-by-side through the grasslands. Suddenly, Johnny pulled up sharply, for a covey of quail had flushed about fifty yards ahead of them. He motioned to Ruth to be quiet and reached for his Winchester. A look of terror formed on Ruth's face, and she pointed to a wolf in the grasses. Johnny's reflexes were quick, and he shot the animal.

He cried to Ruth, "Run for home, Ruth!" A look of panic came into her face as she turned sharply. Several wolves rose out of the grass, but then she saw. These were not animals but men dressed in wolf's clothing. These were the dreaded Pawnee that raided Kiowa villages to steal women and kill sleeping braves at night. Some were tearing away their wolf covering, and their shaven heads with the topknot verified their identity.

Johnny was holding his ground and with rapid fire punished the enemy. He wanted to give Ruth a good head start and then turned the Grulla to follow her. Ruth knew the terrain and let her horse race for her village. She rode directly to Red Hand's lodge, where she screamed "Pawnee!" and pointed toward the area where Johnny was still shooting. Amos and Red Hand called together several braves, and they rode into the direction of the battle.

Superintendent Schmitt was at the post with a half-dozen U.S. troopers when the alarm was given, and the five troopers joined Red Hand while the other trooper rode to his camp for reinforcements. Red Hand only had bows and arrows and was not permitted to have firearms according to the treaty.

As Red Hand rode with a dozen Indians toward the firing, he could hear the trumpet sound the call to arms. The army detail was coming.

Johnny had emptied his gun and was using it to swing at Pawnee as they attempted to unseat him from his horse. His Grulla was bleeding from half a dozen cuts, and an arrow was embedded in her shoulder. She turned to face the enemy and lashed out with her hind feet. A sturdy arm grabbed Johnny's leg, but Johnny splintered the walnut stock of the gun on the Pawnee's head.

A dozen faces were turned toward the Mission as the Calvary Troop accompanied by Kiowa raced to Johnny's aid. The Pawnee gave a cry of rage and fled the field of battle.

Johnny toppled from his Grulla just as his horse collapsed.

•

Light was beginning to flood into his eyes, and he opened his eyes to the circle of faces that surrounded his bed.

There was Red Hand, John Beasley, an army Second Lieutenant, Superintendent Schmitt, Causes to Laugh, Ruth, and John Beasley.

"I believe he's coming to," said the lieutenant. "Son, you really put up a fight out there. Killed eight of them, and there are blood spots leading out of there. Amos, Eagle Feather, and my troops are trailing them back to their village. We need to teach them that they cannot steal and kill as they used to do. You intercepted them before they got to the village."

Johnny had several large knots on his arms and chest where war clubs had struck him. His head was wrapped in linen that was stained in blood. He tried to move but his head throbbed, and he became dizzy.

"He might have a fractured skull, as those war clubs were being swung with might when we rode up," said Amos.

"My horse? Is she all right?" asked Johnny. All the circle looked for someone to speak up.

Finally John Beasley said, "She's dead, son. She fought as hard to protect you as you did to protect her."

Ruth could be heard crying, and Causes to Laugh turned to comfort her daughter.

"Try to keep Johnny awake and not let him fall into a coma," said John Beasley.

Johnny had passed out and was out for three days. When he awoke, he was very hungry and tired.

"Ruth, warm up that soup you made the other day." Ruth left the room in a hurry to thaw out the frozen soup. She sat by his bed and fed him, and he studied her as she spooned the soup into his mouth.

Beautiful brown eyes that expressed sympathy and compassion, her auburn hair was piled on her head, revealing small ears and a beautiful, light brown neck. Her dress was a beaded doeskin, and she was slim and lovely.

"Thank you, Johnny, for fighting for us. You did much to save our village from a surprise attack. I'm so sorry you lost your horse." A tear welled up in the corner of her eyes, and Johnny's heart fluttered. In his mind Johnny was thinking not to say anything to her, for he was full of love for her, but what about Cheryl? She heard a slight groan come from his lips.

"Is the soup too hot?" she asked. Johnny slightly shook his head no. He had to say something.

"Ruth, is it possible to love two girls? I love you, but I've said things to Cheryl that she keeps reminding me that we've said to each other. You're here, and she's so far away and it isn't fair to her for me to say this. Ruth, I love you very much. I love your looks, your hair, but most of all I love your ways and your concern for me. I love you for your concern for other people and your Christian ideas and your work here in the mission."

Ruth sat there with a spoon full of soup in her hand. Her mouth slowly opened as his words became clear to her. "Johnny, I've loved you from the moment I first saw you. When I heard that you had saved my uncle Amos and Eagle Feather, I guess that it started there. I loved you when you fought off the robbers, and mother worked over you. I loved you when we went riding together and how you fought for me and the Mission. I love to hear you sing! Oh, Johnny Ragan, I love you with my whole heart, and I plan to fight Cheryl for your total love!" Tears streamed down her face, and she spilled the soup on his shirt. She bent and with a smile tenderly kissed his lips.

Johnny was awed and stirred by her passion. He looked past her and saw her mother standing in the door. Causes to Laugh had heard it all and smiled at Johnny. She had known that Ruth felt such for Johnny, and tears were in her own eyes.

"I have now committed myself past the point of no return. What will I write to Cheryl?" He didn't speak these words aloud, but they formed in his mind.

"Johnny Ragan, eat some more of this soup and get well fast," said Ruth as she saw her mother standing in the door.

Johnny got well quickly, for he had both Ruth and her mother doctoring him. The dizziness slowly departed, and Cheryl was still writing a letter a day, but Johnny was unable to answer her mail.

CHERYL GETS INVITED TO A MILITARY BALL

Virginia Military Institute at Lexington, Virginia, was burned during the War between the States by Union forces under General David Hunter. The destruction was almost complete, had it not been for several faculty members and especially the efforts of General Smith. Efforts were made to rebuild, and the school was reopened October 17, 1865. By 1884, when William enrolled as a plebe in the school, much had been done to improve the facilities. It would be a while before it would reach its former glory, but it was well on its way.

Being a plebe gave William very few privileges, but he took the hazing in good behavior and submitted to the upperclassmen as all good plebes should. He had heard a lot about the school from his dad and looked forward to the Christmas break so he could journey to Roanoke, which was about forty miles to the southwest, to visit with his sister.

William cherished Cheryl's letters, as she told him about several of her girlfriends who were also attending school at Hollins' College. William got the opportunity to see his sister when V.M.I. had its annual Christmas ball. He invited Cheryl to bring a friend and come north to Lexington for the ball.

William had one of his upper class friends go with him to meet the train. They had pooled their resources and rented a surrey and met the train at the station. Cheryl was thrilled as William, in uniform, stood at attention and introduced his upper-class friend. The uniformed young gentlemen looked extremely sharp and well mannered. He held the doors as well as assisted the young ladies into the surrey. William, the plebe, drove the surrey but was not permitted to speak to either his sister or to get acquainted with Cheryl's selection for William as his date for the ball.

A section of the dormitory had been roped off and was considered off limits for the military and a place where the young ladies would spend the night. Professor's wives served as chaperones, and the proper safety of the young ladies was guaranteed. It was in this part of the dormitory that the ladies unpacked and got out their evening apparel for the ball. The ladies were very excited, as many were attending a ball for the first time, and the school was putting its best foot forward in assuring a great time for classmates as well as professors and their wives.

Cheryl was very well dressed, as Melody had outfitted her for such an occasion and had been extravagant in purchasing an evening dress from New York City. She prepared herself to meet her brother and hurried her friend Sharon Oliver, who was to be William's date for the evening.

They met William near the door to the ballroom, and William was delighted with Cheryl's selection for him. Sharon was a brunette with blue eyes and a winsome smile.

"William and I are twins, and what I like he likes. Believe me, he will adore you." Cheryl smiled at Sharon.

"And who will be your date, Cheryl?" replied Sharon.

William stood at the door at attention beside a very tall captain in the U.S. Army. The captain was dressed in the blue dress uniform of the U.S. Army and smiled as the two ladies approached.

"Cheryl, may I present Captain George Hancock, who is one of my professors and is with the Engineer Corp." The captain was delighted as he took Cheryl's hand in his and bowed to kiss it. He was dark complexioned, had blue eyes, and a small mustache. There was a gold braid at his shoulders and a broad, blue, silk band at his waist and a blue stripe down each trouser leg.

"Delighted to meet you, Cheryl." Cheryl's eyes were enormous, and her light brown hair piled high on her head made her easily the queen of the ball.

William was enjoying the attention of Sharon and not one time did he think of his friend Johnny Ragan.

The string band played a waltz, and the captain led Cheryl onto the floor while William moved awkwardly with Sharon.

When the music stopped, all the upper classmen descended on poor William, and Sharon had all the good dancers she could hope for.

The students, however, knew better than to try to cut in on their professor. The captain held Cheryl tight, and managed dance after dance with her. William suddenly thought of Johnny Ragan and tapped the captain slightly on the shoulder and took his sister from his arms.

"I'm not so sure my grades didn't drop a full letter, but Sis, think of my friend Johnny, will you?"

"Johnny Ragan didn't even enter my mind until you mentioned his name. He hasn't written to me for over a week. I'm not going to let any promise that I made to him interfere with my fun at this ball. Besides, you got me the date with Captain Hancock ... Oh, I mean, George."

"Call him Captain Hancock, Sis! I wonder why Johnny hasn't written. Think he's hurt or something? Sis, I got you a date with the Captain to help my grade," he said, smiling impishly.

"You didn't! Did you? Oh, twin brother, just for that I'll have to decide whether you get an *A* for the night or a *C!*"

"For Johnny's sake, I'll take a *C.*" An upperclassman tapped William on the shoulder, and William stood at attention while Cheryl was swept away. A minute later, the captain had Cheryl in his arms again. William watched as student after student danced with Sharon, and he didn't dare cut in on an upperclassman. Still, she smiled at him as she and her partner danced by, and he stood at attention as they passed.

The last dance gave the plebes the opportunity to dance with the ladies they had invited. William took Sharon in his arms as a waltz was being played. It was remarkable what he had learned by watching the captain.

"Oh William, what a change has come over you! You are dancing like a professional."

He also held her very close, which she likewise enjoyed, and when the dancing stopped her face was flushed, and she smiled at him. William escorted Sharon to her part of the dormitory, where they were met by chaperones, and he simply said good night to her. He saw Cheryl being escorted to a side door by the captain, but William was there before the door was closed.

"Come, Cheryl, I'll escort you to your dorm," said William. The captain turned angrily upon William, then saw who it was and hesitated.

"I'll see her to her dorm," said the captain and turned in that direction.

"You just flunked for the night," whispered Cheryl as she passed her brother. "All for Johnny's sake?" she questioned.

Several upperclassmen were surrounding William as he watched the captain escort Cheryl to a chaperone, who opened the door for her into the young ladies' dorm for the night. William had to answer several questions about his twin sister, as he told them she was attending Hollins College at Roanoke.

William barely got into bed before taps. He lay thinking about Cheryl and her behavior with the captain. He wondered what Johnny would do.

The girls packed up for their return to Roanoke. They all breakfasted together, and William was permitted to kiss both his sister and Sharon on the cheeks. The captain rode to the train in the surrey and embraced Cheryl and kissed her on the lips. Cheryl blushed a deep red and looked helplessly at William. Cheryl didn't invite the caress, and it angered William, who pulled Cheryl from the captain.

"Sir, she is spoken for!" William said. The captain turned a deep red.

"Attention, plebe!" screamed the captain. William stood at attention, and the captain sought another kiss, but Cheryl was prepared and slapped the captain as hard as she could. The blow nearly knocked him off his feet. A look of amazement spread across his face as he watched her kiss her brother good-bye, and she whispered, "You just flunked his course."

"Good girl, that's my twin sister! I love you; you always had a good right cross," he said as he helped his sister and Sharon into the train.

The two girls were joined by others and sat and laughed as they remembered the look that came to the captain's face. When Cheryl told Sharon that the captain was invited so William could get a passing grade in the course Captain Hancock was teaching, Sharon laughed so hard that she held her sides in glee.

Cheryl said, "He'll surely flunk out now!"

Both girls were tired and slept as their train carried them back to Roanoke. Sharon was seeking William's address so she could write him, and Cheryl thought how sharp her date had looked in his captain's uniform. He had earned the slap, but it hopefully taught him that she had scruples, and not every Tom, Dick, or Harry could kiss her without impunity. After all, she thought, she had only been kissed by one man before. Her thoughts went to Johnny as she made comparison of the two men. Right then, Johnny seemed so far away.

The next day, there came a letter from Johnny that told of the Pawnee attack on the Mission and how he'd been injured by war clubs. He had fought to save the women and the missionaries and, although injured, he had beaten off the attack.

Cheryl thought of how she had been untrue to Johnny in thought and had enjoyed the captain's kiss. She loved to dance with the soldier and permitted him to hold her very close. *I surely will hear from Captain George Hancock again. It's only forty miles from Lexington to Roanoke. When I get to know him better, then I will make a selection between Johnny and George.*

A week later she received her first letter from Captain George Hancock. He told her that he was extremely sorry for his behavior and that she had a fine twin brother who will make a very good officer. William had the perfect right to protect his sister and to reprimand him when he sought to take her from the school. George told her that he was a graduate from West Point and that his uncle was General Winfield S. Hancock. The general had run for president of the United States in 1880 but had lost the election. This bit of news shook up Cheryl and overcame any objections that she had in seeing him again. *I must write and tell Johnny that I have found a man that is of interest to me.* She took a pen in her hand and wrote the letter.

•

The next day she received a letter from Johnny, telling her that he had fallen in love with Ruth. Cheryl knew Ruth well and knew of her charm and beauty. Johnny had not spared her but told how Ruth had nursed him to health and had cared for him, and that he was torn apart between his love for Cheryl and his love for Ruth. A tear fell from her fickle eye as she thought of Johnny and her first kiss. She picked up her history book and read of the greatness of General Hancock who was one of the heroes of Gettysburg. *I must write Dad about General Hancock, for he sometimes would talk of the charge of his brigade at Gettysburg and losing so many friends.* Was it not General Hancock who fought against her dad? I'm not going to fight the War between the States in my life but will forgive George for being a Yankee.

Sharon was different and said, "I hate blue! A Yankee will always be a Yankee to me, and my dad fought them as hard as he could. I really enjoyed the battle of Lexington Station, when a Texas girl inflicted physical punishment on the enemy." The southern belle burst out in laughter, much to the chagrin of Cheryl.

"After that first kiss I almost surrendered." Cheryl smiled. "I saw all kinds of flying rockets and explosions."

Sharon laughed. "As the Yankee song goes 'And the rocket's red glare, the bombs bursting in air, gave proof...'" continued Sharon.

"Oh stop it! William gave you a peck on the cheek, remember!" chided Cheryl.

"I wish he had some of the fire his twin sister has." Sharon smiled.

JOHNNY GETS CALLED BACK TO THE TM RANCH

Johnny had completed a full year of study under John Beasley and Thomas C. Battery. He had studied hard and passed the tests given to him at the end of the year.

"Johnny's an intelligent young man, and I know that he could pass exams to enter any college in the country," John said to Causes to Laugh. "He also has the affection of our daughter and isn't getting letters from Cheryl anymore. He's been saving his money, and we can expect him to come to us and ask for the hand of Ruth."

Red Hand had given Johnny an Appaloosa horse to replace the Grulla that Johnny had lost.

"You lost your horse in defending our tribe and the Mission, so it's fitting that I give you my very best horse," said Red Hand. The horse was tan with a tan and white face and Appaloosa cream spots on his rump. The animal was fifteen hands high and extremely powerful. The horse eyed Johnny as Johnny approached him and patted him and showed affection to him. It was but a few days before the horse was following Johnny wherever he went. Johnny kept the horse in the Mission Corral and in the manger.

A letter with a sixty-dollar check came from Thomas McDowell, telling Johnny to return to the ranch because there was some rustler difficulty again. Johnny was to bring Amos and Eagle Feather with him. Johnny approached Amos and read the letter to him and Eagle Feather, for neither could read. Plans were made to begin their trip to the ranch the next morning. Johnny carried the letter to John Beasley to read and pass it on to Causes to Laugh. Ruth watched the effect that the letter had on her parents, and Johnny took Ruth's hand and led her into the room where services usually were held.

"Ruth, darling, I've been called back to the ranch, for they're having rustler difficulty. Amos, Eagle Feather, and I plan to leave in the morning. This is coming at a time in which I'm not fully prepared. I've five hundred dollars, but I fear this isn't enough, but I want an understanding between us. I love you more than life itself and want you to be my wife, but I fear that I've no home to take you to. I can't marry you yet, but I want you to know of my love so that we can make plans."

"Oh Johnny, I love you too. You're dearer to me than anything on this earth. I'll live in a shack, if necessary, but I'll marry you whenever you say."

He held her close and kissed her.

Ruth, with tears in her eyes, quoted from Ruth 1:16, "Intreat me not to leave thee, or return from following thee, for whether thou goest I will go, and where thou lodgest, I will lodge, thy people shall be my people, and thy God shall be my God" (KJV). The scripture was like *dunamis* in Johnny's heart. (The Greek word for *power* used by Paul speaking to the Romans! Romans 1:16.) He must prepare for her and call her to him as soon as possible.

Together, they told Causes to Laugh and John Beasley of their plans to marry, and it would be as soon as they found a home. John and Causes to Laugh were very delighted. They saw in Johnny a young man who loved the Lord and wanted to serve Him. Ruth and Johnny would make a great Christian couple.

The next morning, Ruth was up before dawn to watch her beloved with Amos and Eagle Feather depart for the TM Ranch. Ruth stood, with tears streaming down her face, and waved to him as long as she could see him.

The trip to the TM Ranch was uneventful, and by five o'clock in the afternoon of the fourth day they rode up in front of the bunkhouse. The crew was just coming in, and they all congregated together and dismounted their horses to shake hands and welcome one another. Rex, Slim, and the cook had been back to the ranch for six months, and Rex had not wasted any time in wooing Erma. He finally got up enough nerve to pop the question.

"I didn't think you'd ever get around to asking me! I'd have said 'yes' before you took that trip north; I love you, you big galoot!" Erma grinned.

They'd been married in the hacienda and filed for lands to homestead near a lake that the Mexicans called *Amarillo,* which means yellow in English. The clay, along the banks and shore of the lake, was yellow. The country was wild and well-suited Rex, for he had but few neighbors. He planned to set up a business of taking cattle north to markets on a percentage basis. Slim, the cook, and he had taken the Shawnee Trail for the last time and had to pay more than they could afford to pass the herd through lands homesteaded by carpetbaggers. They fought Indians and nearly lost Andy.

The Good-night-Loving Trail had been blazed by Good-night and Loving into Colorado and the Chisholm trail led herds to Abilene and Dodge City.

Rex enjoyed this type of work and hired a few Mexicans to ride with him and made a good living. Tom McDowell paid him well to take his herds northward, and Matt sent his herd also in Rex's care.

Rex and Erma wasted no time, and he impregnated her the first year. He got a lot of help from the TM Ranch in constructing a home. By the time the baby was born, Rex and Erma had moved into their new home, and a second baby was now on the way. The boy was named Rex Jr. Erma had her son at the hacienda, for the TM Ranch was busy in a round-up prior to Rex making a drive north on the Ogallala Trail.

Tom and Melody's youngest children loved to hold the boy, and Melody was there to spoil him.

Johnny felt right at home as he talked with Andy, Slim, and the cook. Johnny found that the cook was partial to him, for the cook remembered the lasso that had righted the chuck wagon when they crossed the river.

Tom and Melody McDowell had him at the hacienda the evening of his return from the mission, and he sang with George several songs. John Beasley had sent a letter to Tom telling how good a student Johnny had been and of the saving of the Mission by Johnny when he fought the Pawnee and saved the tribe and Ruth. As Tom read the letter, when he came to the part of the Pawnee attack he read it aloud for Melody and George to hear. Johnny blushed as Tom read and then he read of Red Hand's Appaloosa gift to replace Johnny's Grulla.

"Have you heard from William and Cheryl?" asked Tom.

"It's been six weeks since I've heard from Cheryl, but I still get letters about once a week from William, sir," said Johnny. Melody had stopped playing and sat with her head down.

"We were of the opinion that you and Cheryl were writing on a steady basis," said Tom.

"We were, but she found another friend, sir, according to William," said Johnny stiffly.

"So I've heard!" said Tom. "And I'm not too happy about it either! I thought sending her to a girl's college would educate and refine her. This Professor Hancock is a mature man, and he's seeing my little girl. Johnny, what can we do about it?" Melody about fell off her seat at the piano.

"Nothing, sir. I'm engaged to marry Ruth Beasley, and I love her very much. As soon as I can find a home for her, we plan to marry," said Johnny.

"Ruth Beasley, Causes to Laugh's and preacher John Beasley's daughter? Well, I'll be!" remarked Tom. Melody sat very still, and a tear came from her blue eyes. Tom stood and walked the floor, and as he passed Melody he heard her say, "Serves us right for meddling in young lives." Tom stopped pacing and saw the tear on Melody's face.

"Welcome home, Johnny; we're having trouble up north near the line shacks with rustlers and have lost two of our men. We want you, Amos, and Eagle Feather to occupy those three houses, and we'll send patrols at least once a week to back you all up. We're about to complete our annual round-up for Rex to take north and are missing an estimated hundred head of cattle. As soon as the round-up is over, we'll send three more men to work with you."

"Johnny, be careful up there and don't take any chances. Amos and Eagle Feather are good, sound men, so rely on them," continued Tom.

Amos, Eagle Feather, and Johnny spent the next day gathering supplies for the trip north. The cook was helping them plan what they would need, knowing that there were some supplies already in the kitchens of the line shacks. They were all packed and ready to leave the next morning.

Rex rode into the ranch with Cheryl near dusk as the cowboys were at supper. The surrey was filled with luggage, and Cheryl was dressed in a light gray suit with her light brown hair piled on her head.

Melody ran from the hacienda, followed by Tom, and there was a cry of glee as they all embraced one another. Erma come from the hacienda holding her son, and several of the cowboys shouted greetings from the summer kitchen.

Cheryl was more beautiful than the cowboys remembered, for she was now a lady, and there was no sign of her being the tomboy who had left.

Andy turned to several of his friends and said, "Wow, has she changed."

The group stared in bewilderment as they looked at the sophisticated young lady as she hugged her dad and mother. She waved at several of the cowboys and paid attention to Erma and her son.

"Rex, you old sly fox, you won out, for she was the lady to win when I left. How did you beat out George?" asked Cheryl.

"I guess it was my good looks and charm that did it," crowed Rex. Erma smiled at her husband. "It was Rex all the time, but he was too timid to ask me."

"Is Johnny here?" asked Cheryl. "Is he still at the Mission?"

"Hey, Johnny!" called Tom, and Johnny came out of the summer kitchen.

"How do you do, Cheryl?" drawled Johnny and extended his hand in greeting. "You sure look nice—school really made you into a gracious lady."

"Thank you, Johnny! It's good to see you." They looked at each other as Tom and Melody watched to see what effect it would have.

"Have you seen William? Is he well?" asked Johnny to fill in an awkward moment.

"He's fine and doing well at V.M.I.," answered Cheryl. Johnny had filled out and was now a giant of a man. He held his sombrero in his hand, and his black wavy hair hung around his ears. His face was tanned, and his new shirt was tight against his massive chest and arms. Cheryl was comparing him to her captain, and she had a moment of regret, for her captain was a sophisticated snob.

Johnny knew that she didn't know of Ruth, and he found himself comparing this lovely lady with his auburn beauty. Could a man love two women? His mind went back to Ruth, the lovely Indian maiden, and her Christian character.

Cheryl turned toward her parents, and the contest was over. Tom put his arm around his daughter, and Johnny could hear him say, "Now, Cheryl, tell me about this professor Hancock." The door closed, and Johnny didn't hear her answer.

The next morning, Eagle Feather and Johnny mounted and rode to Amos's dwelling, where Amos awaited. It was an exceedingly dry time, and they knew that their dust could be seen for a mile or two. Johnny had named his Appaloosa "Jack," and the stallion moved powerfully along the trail. Johnny patted him and showed affection to the horse, and Jack enjoyed it. Eagle Feather was a man of very few words, and so Johnny rode, thinking of Ruth and where he could find a home for her. Occasionally, his mind went to Cheryl and wondered about the captain and whether anything would come of their romance.

Amos had homesteaded property near to Matt, and a home, built primarily of pine from eastern Texas, had been constructed by the TM Ranch for their lead scout. His wife, Red Doe, half-sister to Causes to Laugh, was full of questions about Ruth. Amos had been home a couple of days, and Johnny wondered why Amos had not answered most of such questions.

"Amos is more Indian than white," Johnny had heard from Tom McDowell and after meeting his wife and their three children, he knew it to be true. Very little conversation was carried on in the family. Her dad, Wolf Fang, was visiting with his daughter, and he would have it no other way but for Eagle Feather and Johnny to sit and smoke the rum tobacco with him. He remembered Johnny's Appaloosa horse as being his sons' favorite horse, and Johnny told him why Red Hand had given the horse to him.

"Praise the Lord!" He smiled. It finally sank in that this was Ruth's grandfather, and he became a very special friend to Johnny. Johnny told him that he planned to marry Ruth, and Wolf Fang really studied Johnny.

"Heap good marriage!" said the old man in broken English. "Raise many children! Follow God's Son! Praise the Lord!" Amos's wife smiled, all said good-bye, and the scouts mounted and rode out, leading the pack horses.

During Johnny's year at the Mission, he had ridden and hunted with Red Hand and now could read signs. Johnny's hearing and eyesight were excellent, and Eagle Feather had learned to show some respect to Johnny for his insight. Amos was losing some of his eyesight, and his hearing was fading also. Neither Eagle Feather nor Johnny had said anything to each other, but both knew that Amos would soon need to retire from scouting. It was too dangerous to scout with dimmed eyesight and without acute hearing.

Eagle Feather rode up front and suddenly dismounted from his horse and stood for a moment and looked at the trail. "Six riders on shod horses were here a day or two ago," said Eagle Feather.

Amos dismounted, and Johnny sat his horse, seeing what Eagle Feather had said to be true. Johnny pointed toward the mountains.

"Shall we follow? There are not enough of them to be military. It's the right size to be rustlers," said Johnny.

"Let's fill our knapsacks with four days' rations, and I'll drive the mules to the Line Shacks and cut your trail between here and the mountains. That way we won't make as much dust and won't be slowed by the pack mules," said Amos.

Johnny and Eagle Feather watched Amos drive the mules toward the line shacks and then turned toward the west and followed the trail of the shod horses. There was no attempt on the rustler's part to cover their tracks, and they appeared to be in no hurry.

There were some paddocks near a box canyon, which was used by the TM Ranch to catch wild horses, and it was well watered and used for a holding pen for broken Mustangs. The six shod horses were making a beeline for the box canyon.

Johnny spoke to Eagle Feather, "Let's approach the canyon from the west, and we can see from the lip of the rim just what's going on."

"Ugh!" Eagle Feature nodded, and they rode to the rim, dismounted, and crawled on their bellies to the rim and looked down. Four wranglers were standing on the top or near the paddock fence and looking at the horses.

Johnny searched for the other two and saw them watching their back trail; they had their rifles in their hands.

Johnny crawled back for his Sharp rifle, shells, and also carried his Winchester. He got back to the rim and could see all six rustlers. They had opened the gate and were in the process of moving the horses out.

"Don't think I would do that, boys! As you can see by the brand, those are TM Ranch horses." All six of the men froze for a minute, and then they moved into action and began pulling their rifles from their rifle boots. Eagle Feather shot one from his horse, and the rustler rolled over the back of his horse. The smoke from Eagle Feather's gun showed the bandits the location of Johnny and Eagle Feather. They began to shower the rim with bullets and moved to cover behind the fence, among the rocks of the canyon.

Johnny, under the rim, moved to his right and had a good shot at one of the bandits. The man dropped his rifle and fell straight away into the rocks. Johnny again moved under the rim to his right and knew that he was now out of range for the Winchester. He loaded the Sharp and slipped the big gun over the rim. He pulled the first trigger and adjusted the rear sight and aimed at a bandit across the canyon who believed he was safe and out of range. The big gun roared, and a second later Johnny heard the spat of the bullet as it struck flesh. The three bandits that were left could not see Johnny but knew he had the big gun. They all stood up, dropped their guns, and lifted their arms straight up in surrender.

"Eagle Feather, climb down while I hold my gun on them and corral them while I come down!" yelled Johnny, and Eagle Feather nodded his head.

Johnny and Eagle Feather had all three men tied up tight when Amos came riding up to the Paddock.

"What's going on here?" asked Amos. He stood looking at the three dead bandits and the prisoners all tied up. He hadn't heard the shooting and looked sheepishly at Johnny when he was told he had missed the fight.

"They were stealing our horses," said Johnny.

"That's a capital offense," said Amos. "We should string them up."

Johnny shook his head no, that he wanted nothing to do with it.

"I'll take them back to Matt and leave them with him. He was a Texas Ranger, you know, and will take them on back to the TM Ranch. Tom will know what to do with them."

"You guys been stealing our cattle too, eh?" asked Johnny, but the three denied that.

"Eagle Feather and I know how to get information the Kiowa way from captives. What do you say, Eagle Feather? You watch them while I build the fire." All three captives turned white as Amos began to gather wood.

"You won't let them burn us will you, sir? You're the only white man among them?" The wood caught fire, and Amos threw his lariat over a limb of an overhanging tree.

"We aren't guilty of rustling, but there are some Indians we've been hiding from and saw them pushing about a hundred head toward the north. They looked like Pawnee with their top knots. That was a good two weeks ago," spoke one of the frightened bandits.

"That figures!" said Johnny. "Now we're in trouble; we need to trail those Indians, and we have these horse thieves on our hands. I guess since you have your lariat over that tree limb, we might as well go ahead and administer justice to them. Hang them high!" The rustlers again turned white as they watched Amos make a noose in preparation for the hanging.

"Sir," said one of the men to Johnny, "if you'd let us out of this, we'll promise to go straight and never rustle horse or cattle. We're homesteaders and not cattlemen and have wives and children."

"Take your friends back to their homes, and let this be a serious lesson to you. You're in Texas now, and we administer justice with a lot of speed," said Johnny. The three gathered their dead friends and were happy to ride out without being hung. After the men rode away, Amos turned to Johnny.

"I hope you don't live to regret that. Tom won't like that, but I'm with you. I hate to see a guy get his neck stretched."

"That big gun kills a long way away," said Eagle Feather. "It was that one shot that made them all give up."

]Johnny nodded agreement.

Amos looked at Johnny then at the Sharp. "What's the purpose of that first trigger?"

"It takes about a four-pound pull to fire this gun, and in doing so you'll pull off to the right every time. That first trigger compensates for the pull and makes the back trigger a hair trigger. Sharpshooters during the war had the double trigger and thus were more accurate," answered Johnny.

"It sure works for you! You're the best shot I've ever seen. Tom McDowell was great with a Winchester and could fire it with accuracy as fast as he could work the lever and shoot. But you can hit a target I can't even see!" said Amos.

"We might as well head to the line shacks and try to find the old trail of those hundred head of cattle. I know where the Pawnee live, and I'm sure Eagle Feather can lead us there," said Johnny. "By the time we decide and have proof of where the cattle are, the round-up should be over, and we can get some help," he added.

JOHNNY IS INVITED TO JOIN THE TEXAS RANGERS

When Tom heard the Pawnee had rustled his cattle, he was angry, and when Johnny told of the Pawnee and their attack on the Kiowa and the Mission, he was almost beside himself. Johnny said the information given by the Rustlers had not been verified, for the trail was too old to be followed by Amos, Eagle Feather, and Johnny, and there was nothing left but to report what he heard to Tom.

"I'll turn this information over to the northern troops or to the Texas Rangers." The Rangers had been restored to power in 1874. The Rangers were still recruiting men, but Matt was no longer interested in being a lawman. He was happy to be with Bess, and he enjoyed ranching.

"What kind of pay do they give?" inquired Johnny. It seemed like sixty dollars a month was a very slow salary to build up his money so he could marry Ruth. He had asked Matt and found that one hundred dollars a month was top pay.

"Can a man be married and be a Ranger?" asked Johnny.

"I was," said Matt, "and had my own house in Big Spring. You'd need to find a house in Texas, though."

"Could I homestead a hundred sixty acres, farm it, and still be a Ranger?" asked Johnny.

"You could try, but you need to have a crop out to homestead, and being a Texas Ranger requires a lot of running, shooting, and traveling."

"I'll write to Ruth and ask her if she would want to try it. I want to marry that girl and don't seem to be any closer than when I left her at the Mission."

"I'm afraid trying to do both will be too much for you. There are a couple places where land is available to homestead. There are 160 acres next to Amos and 160 acres next to Rex, near the Amarillo. Take your pick and file on them. I'll get several of the TM gang to help you put up a house. Tom needs you to stay with him, for you're a trustworthy, hardworking young man, and Tom needs a scout. You know as well as I do that Amos will soon have to give up due to his eyesight and hearing. If you want to try being a Ranger, why not try it part time? I still have some pull in the Rangers, and there are times the Rangers could use some help."

"Thanks, Matt," said Johnny.

He went to the bunkhouse to write his letter to Ruth and lay out the situation to her. Johnny filed on the 160 acres next to Amos, for it was near to the TM Ranch. Ruth would be living next door to her aunt and uncle Amos DeJohn and her three cousins. She would also see her grandfather often, for he loved to spend time with Amos and his daughter, Red Doe.

•

Cheryl had gone back to school, and that was that. William still wrote to Johnny and heard of the fight with the rustlers. He forwarded the story on to Cheryl, but she didn't seem to care. Captain Hancock was spending more time in Roanoke and then asked Cheryl to marry him, just as she was in her sophomore year. She told the dashing young captain that she needed to finish her schooling first, and this somewhat angered him, for few spoke in a negative way to him.

He pouted for a month and then came back to see her with the news that he would soon make major. She told him that her dad had been a major in the Confederate Army, and when he found out that Tom had been with the Kemper brigade, he told her that his brother had defeated the whole Division and almost completely destroyed it at Gettysburg. This angered Cheryl, so she went into the dorm of the school and slammed the door in his face. Two weeks later she relented and wrote an invitation to him to visit her again. He came in a surrey and took her for a ride among the beauty of the Blue Ridge Mountains, and among the flowering dogwood trees, kissed her, and asked her to marry him again.

"Captain Hancock, the answer is yes, but we must wait until I have graduated. You don't want to be married to a girl who has no degree. I'll be out in two years."

The captain called William in and informed him that he was engaged to his sister. William was an upper classman at V.M.I. and no longer had the captain as his professor. Most of the upperclassmen hated the captain, for he was a Yankee, and the Civil War was still being fought in the classrooms and halls of the buildings. Most of the students were children of veterans who had fought for the south and didn't care for the captain or his brother.

One night a group of southern upperclassmen dressed up like the KKK and caught the captain in the surrey, coming back from Roanoke, and tarred and feathered him. The tar was hot and blistered him; the blisters burst when he attempted to rid himself of the tar. He was totally put out by the deed, and called up several southern boys before the college professors and tried to find out just who the KKK members were. The group had sworn to secrecy, and no one found out who was responsible. The captain remembered how angry Cheryl had been when she found out that her dad had lost to the captain's uncle. He called William before the professors and though William denied it, the captain claimed William was a KKK member and told of the reaction of Cheryl.

William declared on his honor that he had not done such a thing and knew no one who had been responsible. The court of professors (some smiling as they did) was closed, and the KKK members remained unknown. The entire senior class had all cleaned out tar from under fingernails and the captain remained a joke to all the upper class.

William took his pen and wrote the full story to his dad and to Cheryl. His dad wrote angry letters to the college that threatened to cut off his finances for the school. Apologies were returned to Tom from the college. Cheryl reacted differently. She threw his engagement ring at him and once more slammed the door to the dorm in the captain's face.

Two weeks went by, and Cheryl sent no letters to him. He wrote her several apologies, but Cheryl gritted her teeth and finally returned his letters to him unanswered. The Confederate Belle had won the battle at Roanoke. Sharon knew the story from William and rejoiced at Cheryl's reaction.

"That egotistical nincompoop got just what he deserved." She smiled at Cheryl.

Now the captain was living hard for the general staff at the college reviewed the case, and the captain did not make major. They passed over him for promotion and gave the position to another.

The captain complained to his uncle, and he was transferred away from V.M.I. to the Oklahoma Territory and action against the Indians. William wrote his dad and sent a letter to his sister, telling of the transfer. Cheryl wondered if she had done the right thing in rebuking the captain. Her mind went back to Johnny, who was now the head scout at the ranch due to Amos's aging.

Johnny was homesteading 160 acres next to Amos, and each evening several of the cowboys would meet on the homestead and work on building a new house for Johnny and Ruth. There were a couple good carpenters among them, and they used the rest of the crew as carpenter's helpers. Matt brought his crew of four and added to the labor force. Tom McDowell and Melody rode out and brought the chuck wagon with them, and the cook worked on cooking while the TM crew worked joyfully at constructing a large, three-bedroom home.

Johnny saw the need and bought a circular saw, which was powered by water on the Canadian River, and hauled logs to the mill. He hired several of the Kiowa from the Mission, and John Beasley came down and showed them how to saw lumber. This mode of employment was very popular with the Indians, and several of the Indians took pride in their work.

John Beasley studied the lumber business and brought in planing equipment and built a large kiln to season the wood, and finished lumber was soon being produced. Homesteaders from miles around came to see the mill, and soon it became a flourishing business. The Indians became productive in cabinet making and worked various designs into the wood.

Tom McDowell was so pleased that he donated five acres of his ranch to Johnny for "his project," and Johnny called on John Beasley to supply the labor. Woodworking became one of the courses offered at the mission, and Amos, now without work, decided he was too young (sixty) to sit around the house and went to the Mission and took the course. Amos took to woodworking with a special zeal and drew up several Kiowa designs, which the Indians enjoyed etching into the wood. The project was a huge success, and Johnny shared his good fortune with the Mission.

The house was completed, and Johnny sent to Big Spring for six gallons of light green paint and two gallons of white, and the last of his hoarded money went to buy furniture and various odds and ends so Ruth and he could get married and set up housekeeping.

Ruth came and visited her aunt (Amos's wife,) and together they measured and made curtains and quilted quilts. The Mission added several Kiowa women to helping with the quilting, and Causes to Laugh set up classes at the Mission for the project and the making of pottery. A kiln was produced by Mr. Battery, and Kiowa designs were glazed into the objects. The Mission grew in prosperity, and the tribe took pride in its handicraft.

Causes to Laugh approached her husband and told him of the Thanksgiving dinner that Tom McDowell had shared with the Kiowa nearly twenty years ago and suggested to the Missionary that such a feast would be very popular in the light of their recent prosperity. The Missionary considered it a very good idea and took the idea to Red Hand, who well remembered the dinner so many years ago.

"We shall have such a feast and give our glory and honor to Jesus Christ, our Lord who is the author of our prosperity." Red Hand smiled.

Ruth approached Johnny and asked if the marriage could not be held at the Mission, at Thanksgiving time, when the feast was being enjoyed by all. Johnny was reluctant at first, for he hoped that the marriage could be held at the house, now completely finished, but Ruth wanted to be married at the Mission.

Tom and Melody McDowell hitched up their surrey and, accompanied by their cowboys and chuck wagon, rode to the Mission. Ruth invited the U.S. Army as well as the full settlement to feast with the Mission. The army, not to be outdone, furnished their mess hall, and their cooks joined with the cook from the TM Ranch and cooks from the mission to produce a tremendous thanksgiving meal.

Red Hand gave a speech of praise and thanksgiving, and the army chaplain added a few words, followed by John Beasley of the Mission. Tom McDowell gave the prayer of Thanksgiving, and the meal was brought out by several from the army.

The colonel spoke a few words relative to the peace of the world, and all said, "Amen." Everyone enjoyed the meal.

Following the meal, John Beasley solemnized the marriage of Ruth and Johnny. Ruth was beautiful in a gown of white, with a white veil. Johnny was dressed in a dark blue broadcloth suit. They stood facing each other.

"I, Johnny, take thee Ruth to be my wedded wife, to have and to hold, from this day forward ... " Her smile gave way as a large tear came from her right eye. Still she would not, and could not, keep her eyes from her beloved. He thought she might have trouble with the oath, but she spoke clear and sweet, looking him straight in the eye. "I, Ruth, take thee Johnny, to be my wedded husband, to have and to hold from this day forward, for better, for worse ... "

They exchanged rings, and John Beasley said, "Now I pronounce you husband and wife; what God hath joined together let no man put asunder."

A long row of cowboys were in line to kiss the bride and to congratulate Johnny. There were Indians, calvary officers, cowboys, and Johnny's lumbermen all present to wish the young couple the greatest of happiness.

Johnny and Ruth spent their marriage night at the mission and slept in Ruth's bedroom, where the marriage was consummated. They had an early breakfast with the cowboys at the army's mess hall and started the five-day journey to their new home and the hacienda.

Tom and Melody McDowell gave the couple a ride back to Johnny's new house. Johnny tied his Appaloosa to the back of the surrey and sat in the back with Ruth as she looked at him, and they held each other tight.

Ruth had not seen the house since it had been painted and was amazed at what the two coats of paint did to the beauty of the structure. Johnny lifted his bride, carried her over the threshold, and kissed her.

"Welcome home, honey," said Johnny. "You'll want to rearrange the furniture, but I did the best I could. Let me go out and put the horse in the barn."

The luggage was all unpacked when Johnny came back in, and Ruth was standing in the living room studying the room. "I do believe that I'll put that chair over there."

In the kitchen, she was amazed to find a pump so she could have water in the house.

"Oh Johnny, I just love all of the thinking that went into the construction of our home." She stood looking at the Indian rug on the kitchen floor. "My grandmother did this?"

"Both grandmothers! And your aunt, Amos's wife, helped quilt the five quilts in the closet in the hall."

"Melody and Tom gave us that grand piano, for they wanted us to sing His praises and enjoy music as they enjoy it each evening," said Johnny.

"Dad taught me to play while I was a child, and as you know I play at the Mission," said Ruth. She sat at the piano and played and sang in an alto voice, "Praise God, from who all blessings flow, praise Him all creatures here below, praise Him above ye heavenly hosts, praise Father, Son, and Holy Ghost." Johnny sat down and joined her, and then they turned towards each other.

"Johnny, this is the happiest day of my life."

●

Johnny rode to the sawmill, where he met a couple of men dressed in gray suits.

"I'm George Wilson, and this is Aaron Lamp. We represent the Atchison, Topeka, and Santa Fe Railroad. We've been buying right of way through here and have bought from Mr. Tom McDowell, right of way into New Mexico. We'll be constructing railroads and will be felling trees and would like to get a contract with you to saw railroad ties for us. We'll pay eighteen cents apiece to saw them. We'll haul the trees to you and will haul the ties by railways to the work site. We'll need to build a spur to your mill."

Johnny sat stunned, for he had no idea how much income this would produce for the Mission and himself. John Beasley was at the mill, so Johnny called him into the mill office and asked him what he thought of the offer. John sat and estimated about $3.20 a tree.

"Let's do it!" Johnny agreed. The mill began almost overnight, and for a while, as the spur was being constructed, the ties were hauled by wagon to the construction site. Amos was put in charge of this work, and he did it well.

Johnny worked for Tom but often was at the mill, as John Beasley needed to be at the Mission. Lumbering was hot work and the mill needed to be kept in good working order.

Johnny added a pitch vat and immersed the raw ties in heated pitch. Johnny was paid an extra fifteen cents for this so that when completed the tie cost the railroad $.33 a piece or about $436.00 each mile. Overnight Johnny and the Mission made hundreds of dollars. But this was only the beginning, as many more got into the lumber business, and now that the spur was in place there was railcar after railcar of lumber sitting on the tracks, waiting to be sawed into lumber and in many cases to be finished. The kiln was kept burning night and day as the raw wood was seasoned into finished lumber.

Johnny rode into the hacienda on his Appaloosa and was heralded by various cowboys. He rode to the front of the hacienda and tied his horse to a metal loop on a post. He knocked at the door.

"Get that, will you, Cheryl?" called Melody, and Cheryl and Johnny stood looking at each other.

"Cheryl, I had no idea you were home from school." Johnny broke the silence as they continued to look at each other. She was dressed in a riding habit and blouse. Her brown hair was piled on her head, but two earrings hung from her ears. Her cheeks were flushed, and suddenly she became aware that she was staring at Johnny, and Johnny was staring at her.

"I'm finished with school. I graduated last month. I've been home for two whole days," she continued. "How is Ruth?"

"She's fine! Thanks." Johnny smiled. "Is your dad in?"

"Yes, come in; he's in the study." She led the way to the study, where she knocked on the door and Tom McDowell appeared.

"Hello, Johnny, how's Ruth, and how are things at the Mill?"

"Ruth's great and things couldn't be any better at the mill." Cheryl turned to leave, and Johnny said, "Good to see you again, Cheryl."

"Tom, I need another ten acres from you, if you would sell it to me. We have lumber piled sky high all over that five-acre tract, and we haven't enough room," said Johnny. "That isn't the reason for my call, but I wanted to talk to you later about the land. Tom, I can no longer do two jobs, and I feel that Eagle Feather would make you a great chief scout. We haven't had any more trouble with rustlers since I killed the last ones, and I need to be at my mill helping Amos."

"Been looking for you to come to see me, as I knew that you had outgrown your job with me. Johnny, you are a remarkable young man, and you've been a great help to me. Your influence with William really made him into a man. You know that he's graduated and is a second lieutenant in the army and will be there for four years. He'll make a great engineer when he gets out. His regiment is in Oklahoma working with the railroad," continued Tom. "I'll sell you the extra ten acres at five dollars an acre. I believe that it's worth fifty dollars an acre, as it's adjacent to your railroad spur," said Tom.

"I'll pay you the fifty dollars an acre," said Johnny. "Do you know that would be nearly a year's work just a year or so ago? Land is really getting to be valuable. Let me tell you of something that might be of interest to you," he continued. "Harry Sanborn and Joseph Glidden have constructed a town on some lowlands or in flood plains and will be moving the whole town soon. I have bought several lots along Polk Street, and there are many more lots available. This new town will be called Amarillo because of the yellow dirt around the lake. Rex and Erma live near the site chosen for the city. I think they may have an ideal location."

"I'm mindful of the moving and glad that you brought me up to date. I'll have my lawyer see if there are any good lots available," Tom said.

"I plan to open a lumber yard in that area and ship a lot of treated wood for house and business construction. Would you have any qualms about financing such an enterprise? I need some ready cash. I need ten thousand dollars right now but may need to draw extra cash later. I'll pay you three percent interest and might be able to go to four percent later," added Johnny.

"Where did you get your knowledge in economics?" asked Tom.

"Mr. Battery at the Missions taught me, and I studied hard," said Johnny.

"I'll go to fifty thousand dollars, but I have other funds tied up right now," said Tom.

Cheryl was at the door, out of sight, but listening to their conversation. She walked deeper into the room as Johnny came out of the study.

"Good-bye, Cheryl; come over to see Ruth. We live next to Amos and his wife," said Johnny. He donned his sombrero and mounted his horse, tipped his hat, and rode for home.

"What a very fine young man he is, and he's more intelligent than I thought he would be. He's really going to make something out of his life," said Tom as he came out of the study.

"I sure had a crush on him at one time," answered Cheryl.

"I stuck my hand into something that I should not have and separated you two. Cheryl, hindsight is much better than forethought."

"Dad!" yelled Cheryl. "Stop that! He's married now, and she's such a sweet lady."

•

Tom mailed Rex and Erma, telling of the information that he had about the founding of the new city of Amarillo. He told Rex to buy some of the lots, for they would be of value someday.

Within a month's time, there was a new Lumber Company with a city going up about it. "Ragan's Lumber Company" also got into the brick and block business, with Johnny finding clay that made various-colored brick.

Johnny moved into the business area and bought a corner property, where he began a mercantile store.

In six months, he had paid Tom the fifty thousand dollars he had borrowed. In the next four years Johnny Ragan became a millionaire and owned three lumber yards, a bank, and several mercantile stores. He moved into an apartment in a hotel that he owned and would travel back to his house near Amos. Ruth was always the same, and his love for her continued to deepen.

Ruth and Johnny tried several times to have children, but she could not carry one to term, and she usually aborted them in the second month of her pregnancy. The loss of her little ones played a sad note into her life, and Ruth was despondent and grieved over her lost children. She spent extra time at the Mission and tried to immerse herself in her Lord's work. She played for the Mission and taught various classes to the Indian tribe. Her uncle Red Hand loved her like a father loved his daughter, and she was near when Wolf Fang died.

The old chief had slowly lost weight, and though he tried to be cheerful, his smile slowly faded. He would sit and smoke his peace pipe and talk of the peace that he had in his heart since he found Jesus Christ as his personal savior. The Spirit of the Lord was in his heart, and he wanted all to know how he felt.

One day, as Ruth read of Jacob and Joseph from the book of Genesis, she noted how Joseph had brought Jacob, his dad, before the Pharaoh. Jacob had blessed Pharaoh and Pharaoh had asked Jacob, "How old are you?"

Jacob said, "The days of the years of my pilgrimage are a hundred thirty years; few and evil have the days of the years of my life been and have not attained unto the days of the years of the life of my father's in the days of their pilgrimage."

The old chief sat and thought awhile. "What is a pilgrimage?" he asked Ruth.

"A pilgrimage is a person's journey to some sacred or holy place as an act of religious devotion."

The old chief said, "We, as a people, used to travel to the old Sundance grounds at Bear Butte. I know that was pagan and not the worship of the true God."

"Granddad, you're a pilgrim here on earth, and you're just passing through. This world is not your home, but soon you will be going to an everlasting home, made and created for you by Jesus Christ," spoke Ruth.

The old chief sat and thought a moment then softly said, "Praise the Lord! Very soon I meet big Chief soon now that I'll meet Him face-to-face, and my pilgrimage here on earth will be over. My peace comes by knowing Him, peace pipe no good. I no longer smoke my peace pipe but have found peace and joy in knowing and trusting in Him." Wolf Fang smiled as he spoke.

That night Wolf Fang died in his sleep, and the tribe lamented him for several days. John Beasley had the funeral service, and Wolf Fang had many visitors come to participate in mourning the death of the chief. Tom and Melody came from the hacienda with all of their cowboys. Amos and Red Doe, his wife, were there as well as Rex and Erma. Johnny rode into the Mission area, where he met Red Hand. Ruth sat by his side as they together all mourned the death of the great chief. John Beasley, who had overheard Ruth's talk about pilgrimage, used that verse and told of Wolf Fang, the pilgrim, who went home.

Johnny held his wife to him as she mourned for her granddad. They had been separated for almost two weeks, and Johnny felt as if they were slipping apart.

"Ruth, honey, please go back with me for a few days. We need some time together."

"I'm afraid that you will insist we sleep together, and you'll impregnate me again, and I'll lose another child. Johnny, it just tears the heart out of me when I lose one. Is God punishing us for something that we've done? I've prayed and prayed about it and searched my heart and soul; I find nothing in my life that might cause it." She raised her eyes as she spoke, and they lingered on him.

"Honey, you aren't accusing me of causing our children to be aborted are you? This grieves me very much, but I've done nothing amiss except that I've killed twelve men in line of duty to save others. Could it be that? God forbid! I've tried to talk to your dad about it. I've prayed many times about those I've killed, and all needed killing or they would have killed people that I was hired to protect." Johnny put his head into his hands, and his body heaved as he wept.

Ruth drew away from him and whispered, "That's it! That has to be it, for there isn't anything else. Have you been faithful to me while you are away? Are you lusting for another? Are you around Cheryl much?"

Johnny stood up and looked with anger at his wife. "Ruth, I made a vow before God that I would be true to you, and I've kept it fully. Honey, don't anger me in this, for neither one of us has done anything that might cause this!"

"Johnny, don't ask me to go with you, for I can't be a wife to you feeling as I do."

The next morning Ruth remained in bed as Johnny got up and departed for his work in Amarillo. She didn't say good-bye, but after he departed she lay and wept in her pillow. Finally, when she went to breakfast, Causes to Laugh saw her red eyes and tried to find out the cause of her sadness.

"Why didn't you go with Johnny? Didn't he want you?" inquired Causes to Laugh. It was more than Ruth could bear, and she sobbed on her mother's shoulder.

"Ruth, honey, so many women have various difficulties. Your grandmother, my mother, couldn't conceive at all. Years went by, and she tried so many times to become a mother. She thought that she was barren, and she couldn't have a child. The women of the tribe laughed at her and made fun of her. It was almost more than she could bear. She prayed, but it was to a pagan god that she prayed. She fasted and then she ate too much. Nothing happened! Then, suddenly, she was with child, but she almost lost the child because she was afraid that she would abort it just as you do. Finally, she came to herself and said, 'If the great Spirit wants me to bear a child, I will bear a child. If I lose this child, it will be because the great Spirit wills it.' My mother stopped worrying about it and regained her strength, and her food agreed with her. I was born, and mother was so very happy that she named me, 'Causes to Laugh' because my birth was such a blessing to her.

"Now Ruth, the next time that you are with child, trust in the good Lord and put your life and that of the child's in His hands. Eat right and believe that God will bless you and Johnny, and He will."

"Oh Mother, I see the wisdom in what you're saying, but I've offended Johnny and accused him of being untrue to me. It angered him, and I've not seen him so angry. I accused him of being unfaithful with Cheryl. He told me that he loved her and me at the same time before we were married," whispered Ruth.

"Didn't he want you to go with him for a few days?" asked Causes to Laugh.

"Yes, Mother, but I was afraid that I might get pregnant again. Mother, it just kills me to lose a child. I can't stand it! I've been thinking of leaving him and divorcing him," cried Ruth.

"Have you talked to your dad about it? Maybe he can give you some advice," suggested Causes to Laugh.

•

Johnny rode the Appaloosa into the fast-growing town of Amarillo. His lumberyards were very productive, and his bank and mercantile stores continued to grow. But Johnny wasn't happy. Still, he immersed himself in his work and became very prosperous. He was a very handsome young gentleman, and not seeing Ruth by his side caused people to talk, and several women tried to get him alone. He was the catch of the town, thought several, and men tried to set him up with blind dates, and women kept throwing themselves at his feet. He was watchful and managed to keep himself true to Ruth.

One morning he was at the freight station checking on some incoming logs when he ran into a young second lieutenant. The lieutenant had his back to Johnny, and both turned at the same time.

"Well, I'll be! Johnny Ragan! Am I ever glad to see you!" said William McDowell. "Boy, do you look good! Tell me, I see Ragan bank, Ragan Mercantile Stores, Ragan Lumber Company, Ragan brick yard, Ragan Hauling, and have I missed any? Are all of these yours?"

"They're mine!" Johnny said, laughing.

"That course I gave you in economics really paid off didn't it?" laughed William.

"Well, Mr. Battery taught a little too. I owe it all to the good Lord," said Johnny.

"How is Ruth?" asked William.

"I don't know! Haven't seen her in three months now, and it may be over for us, for I hear that she's filing for divorce. She claims that I've been untrue to her, but she knows better than that. William, I'm beside myself not knowing what to do. She's lost three children by not being able to carry them to term and doesn't want to be married anymore. She's afraid she will become pregnant again and lose another child. I've written several letters to her and her dad, but he says he's talked with her, and she would rather remain without a husband than take the chance and lose another baby."

"That's tough! Have you taken her to a doctor?" asked William.

"I have asked her dad to take her to one, but she doesn't want to go. He says she's ashamed of herself and her fears." answered Johnny. "If she wants a divorce, what can I do but pay for it? I can't make her stay married to me. Ruth and I were very happy, I thought, when we first got married, and we lived there by Amos. I even said I would move back there, but she refused. How are your dad and mother and Cheryl? That younger brother and sister must be really growing by now."

"Mom and Dad are fine, and Cheryl is working in Houston, as she wanted city life in lieu of the ranch. My younger brother and sister are doing fine and both are cowboys. Ha!"

"What you doing out here, William?" asked Johnny.

"I'm in charge of a detail to guard the railroad from Indian attack. The Apache have been out of their reservation and appear to dislike the train and all it stands for. I've been here for a month and don't cherish this type of work. The railroad is the hottest place on earth, and we have to keep watch all the time. We know they're there, but we seldom see them, and when we do it's usually too late. I've lost two men since I've been here, and both didn't know what hit them."

"Be careful, friend!" said Johnny. "When and if you get some time off then drop in here and bathe, for my hotel will treat you well. You can spend some time in a real bed too."

"Thanks, Johnny! Well, I've got to get going. I'll drop by periodically. I'll pray for Ruth," said William.

"And I'll pray for you, William. Watch out and keep yourself safe."

William turned and joined two soldiers who were mounted and waiting for him. One held his horse for him while he mounted. He grinned and saluted Johnny. The detail rode through the dust of the street, and Johnny stood and watched William lead his troop.

Johnny rode his Appaloosa into the Mission and tied the horse to a hitching rail. He was quiet, as there might be a service being conducted in the assembly room. He rapped lightly on the massive door, and Causes to Laugh opened the door. For a second she stood, and then she grabbed Johnny and embraced and kissed him.

"My son, you are so handsome. You look so fine! I am so glad to see you. Welcome!" She hugged him again, and Johnny embraced her with true feeling.

John Beasley came from the assembly room with outstretched hand, and Johnny felt the power of his grip. His smile indicated how pleased he was to see Johnny.

"Welcome, son!" said John and embraced Johnny with a Christian hug. "Come on into the house."

"God bless you two," said Johnny. "How is Ruth?"

"We're very worried about Ruth, for she hasn't been herself for a month now. All she wants to do is sleep in the day, and she can't sleep at night, but we can hear her walking in the Mission here and there. She has overeaten and has gained a lot of weight. You know,

Johnny, Ruth has always been very active, but now she seems to have lost interest in everything. John has talked to her and prayed with her, but she's very quiet and holds what is bothering her to herself. We're at a loss as to what to do. She's divorcing you. We both feel that she loves only you and no one else. We were praying that you would come and promised her that we wouldn't write and ask you here. God has brought you here to us and to her too," said Causes to Laugh.

"I've come, as I have her letter wanting me to come. She said that the divorce will be final but that there are some papers that need to be signed," said Johnny. John and Causes to Laugh both showed expressions of sadness. All three turned as they heard the door to her room open.

Johnny caught his breath, for he saw that Ruth was not well. She had gained a good thirty pounds, and her face was swollen. Her eyes were red from crying. When she saw Johnny she stopped and stared at him.

"Oh," she declared, staggered, and would have fallen had not Johnny rushed to her. He held her in his arms, but she stiffened and looked angrily at him.

"Don't touch me! I am no longer your wife! I have some papers that need to be signed." She pulled away from him, and Johnny stood stunned and looked from John to Causes to laugh.

"Ruth, could we talk in private?" asked Johnny.

"What you say to me you can say before my dad and mother," said Ruth.

"I'll sign whatever paper that makes you happy, but as you know, I do not want this divorce. Don't love anyone else. I love only you and want you to be happy," said Johnny.

"I'll be happy when it's all over and the divorce is final. I won't have to live up to the responsibility of being a wife. You'll be free to pursue happiness with another, and this terrible weight will be lifted from my shoulders," said Ruth.

"Ruth, I have no plans to pursue anyone. You've been a good wife, and when you lost those three children, I felt the loss too. They were our children, and they were conceived in marriage and with joy and happiness. Ruth, you were a good wife and need not to be ashamed, for this happens to many. I don't want the divorce but want you to remain my wife," stated Johnny.

"What I have done, I have done. Here are the papers; sign them please," she turned and rushed back into her room. Johnny stood with head down for a full minute and then turned to Causes to Laugh and John Beasley.

"I'm very sorry but that's all that I can do. I'll sign the papers, as the signing appears to be what she wants and her way of solving this problem. I'll mail you a check each month for her care and one for the Mission here. God has blessed me materially, and I see no better way of spending my money than to give a portion of it to this Mission. You two are very special to me. God bless and goodbye!" Johnny signed the papers, turned his back on them, mounted his horse, and rode out of their lives.

Johnny rode four days South, thinking of the house he had constructed for Ruth. No one had lived there for several months, and he feared that it might be in need of repair.

He rode by his homestead and checked to make sure it had not been burglarized. The place was as they had left it. He packed up what personal things belonged to him. Ruth had removed all her things. His heart was in his throat, and tears came to his eyes as he remembered all the good times that Ruth and he had enjoyed living there. Ruth had never had a place like that, and her skill in matching colors as well as curtains were there. Grass was beginning to make the place look untidy, as no one had cut the grass in the yard. Cattle had kept the grass mowed in the fields. He saw cattle that belonged to Matt and some TM Ranch cattle in the fields.

He rode on to the home of Matt and Bess, and they were glad to see him. They showed a lot of concern when he told them of Ruth and the divorce. He offered to sell his homestead to them, as it lay adjacent to their property.

"I'll sell the entire property, including the furniture and personal belongings for two thousand dollars," said Johnny,

Matt wouldn't agree, and said it was worth much more than that and added another five hundred dollars to the price. Johnny finally agreed, and the check was written to Ruth Ragan, and

Johnny made out a bill of sale. Bess had one of her famous meals, and Johnny was hugged by Bess and Matt as he left.

"I have a letter here for you Johnny. It's from my former colonel in the Texas Rangers. You remember that you showed interest in joining the Rangers when Ruth and you lived at your homestead?"

Johnny read the letter, which was an invitation to join the Rangers as a lead scout. Johnny shook his head and turned to Matt. "Matt, when I showed interest in the Texas Rangers, I was interested in making enough money so I could marry Ruth, as you recall. My financial status has brightened considerably, and I now have no interest in hunting men. That tribe of Indians that rustled TM cattle needed to be taught a lesson, but I believe they were in the Oklahoma territory, and there was nothing that the Texas Rangers could do. William is with the calvary up there, and it's up to William to punish them," said Johnny.

"You're going to stop by the TM Ranch, aren't you?" asked Matt.

"Yes, I look forward to seeing every one of them again," said Johnny.

"Cheryl's home right now. She's on vacation and has been out riding every day. She's been by here almost daily. Cheryl's unchanged, although she isn't a child anymore," said Matt.

Johnny said good-bye to Matt and Bess and mounted his Appaloosa for the ride to the ranch. The ranch was much the same except there were some improvements made to paddocks and a new barn with more modern hay equipments for loading hay into the loft. Johnny sat for a moment and studied the new equipment. There was a rail along the interior apex of the barn, which was equipped with pulleys and ropes. An entire wagonload of hay could be forked and lifted by horse to the rail and then would be carried to an area where the fork was tripped and the load would fall at the designated area.

The cowboys would like that, for they always dreaded lifting hay over their heads when filling the barns.

It was about four in the afternoon, and the cowboys would be coming in around five o'clock. Johnny rode past the bunkhouse and approached the hacienda. The cook came out, and Johnny was met with a smile, a hug, and a hardy slap on the back.

"It's good to see you, boy! Aren't you ever going to stop growing? You really look great, and everyone will be glad to see you. I'll call the boss!" He turned and went into the house while Johnny tied his horse. Johnny had the feeling that someone was watching him, and he turned to find Cheryl staring at him as she had done when he first met her, six or seven years ago.

"Hi, cowboy!" She rushed forward with an outstretched hand, and Johnny was surprised when she stood on tiptoes and kissed him on the cheek. Johnny embraced her and then held her at arm's length to look at her.

"You look just like your mother, Cheryl, and I don't know a more beautiful woman than she," drawled Johnny. Johnny was again surprised as Cheryl blushed.

"Flattery will get you everywhere." She smiled. "Johnny, you just look great! I hear that you've been doing very well in business. How is Ruth? Any little ones yet?"

"Ruth divorced me, Cheryl. I just signed the papers earlier this week." Johnny dropped his head as he spoke.

"Oh Johnny, I'm so very sorry." Her dismay was written on her face, and there were questions there also, which she would not ask. Johnny decided to tell her the full story and did.

"You mean that she divorced you because she was afraid?" she asked in alarm. "The poor girl! Johnny, does she still love you?"

"I'm not sure. What she's done has just torn our love for each other into fragments."

"Do you think it would help if Mother or I would talk to her? I've known girl friends that have had the same problem ,and then the first child lives and everything is all right."

"Ruth would not want advice from you, Cheryl, but maybe your mother might help her. Ruth knew about us when you were away to school, and when I've been away on business has accused me of seeing you."

"Johnny, I'm so sorry!"

"Ruth had three miscarriages in three years, and each time she was horrified by what happened," said Johnny sadly. "It hurt me too! I had decided to give her time, but that seemed to be the worst thing that I could do. She got the opinion that I should marry another because she could not be a mother."

"How sad! Ruth is such a very pretty girl and has such a lovely way about her. She always wanted to put others before herself. Bless her!" said Cheryl.

Melody and Tom were at the door.

"Don't make him stand out here, Cheryl; have him come in," invited Tom. As Johnny tied his horse, Cheryl was telling her mother and dad what Johnny had told her, and by the time Johnny entered the hacienda, both parents knew of Johnny's divorce and his trouble with Ruth. Melody was completely white, and Tom looked stunned, for both had known Ruth from the time she had been born.

"How very terrible," whispered Melody. "Johnny, couldn't you have just refused to sign those papers?"

"I tried that, but it didn't work," said Johnny. "I won't put pressure on her but will see what some time away from her will do." Tom agreed, and finally Melody told Johnny that she understood.

"Do you really think she no longer wants to be married to you, or do you think she has done this to give you the freedom so that you may pursue another?" asked Melody.

"That's exactly what she told me!" said Johnny. "Where I live there are so many nice girls; it is very tempting to let her plan work. Maybe when she hears that I'm dating, it may cause her to have second thoughts. After all, I'm just an average guy and get terribly lonely for female companionship."

Cheryl squirmed some. Her dad looked at his daughter, for of all the men that he knew he would rather have Johnny pursuing his daughter than anyone else. Johnny had so completely surprised him that seldom a day went by that he didn't think of the mistake they'd made in separating the two. Melody had the same feeling, for she looked with guilt at her husband.

"Johnny, please stay the night here with us; in fact, spend several days here, and maybe we can help you."

Johnny had several changes of clothing that he had picked up as he went by the homestead. They were basically older work clothes, and there were some buckskin scouting clothing.

"I sold my homestead to Matt when I went by his house, so I'm burning my bridges behind me," said Johnny sadly. "The way I feel right now, I may never get married again. I won't be able to stay more than a day, for I have my own businesses and have few that I trust to carry on the work while I'm away. Amos is working with me, and I know that his work in logging will be done right. I now have five mills, and the volume of business continues to grow. The railroad has brought into this area hundreds and thousands of new residents, and new cities are springing up. I've founded masonry kilns and have three construction companies with two more being planned as carpenters become available. I've five hauling companies that have been hauling from railroad stations to deliver goods. I have two banks and plan several more and need bank managers and employees. My mercantile stores have multiplied so that I'm building one a month, but my need is for honest, good employees. I have several full-time employees that are keeping books for me, and I've had to fire a few dishonest men and have had to imprison a few for stealing. I would give William a good partnership in my construction companies, if he were free. I've thought of him several times."

Tom sat amazed and could hardly believe what he was hearing. Johnny was growing by leaps and bounds, and it would be difficult to try to estimate just what he was worth. God was behind it all, and clearly His hand could be seen in the life of Johnny. Cheryl sat enchanted as she thought of her past and the letters she had mailed to this man and the mistakes she had made.

"Johnny, those trying to rob you, are they threatening bodily harm? I could loan you Slim for a while. I've never seen a person who could use a six gun any better than he."

"I have the Pinkerton Detective Agency working for me through the railroad. I own a controlling amount of stock in two railroad systems. I can rely on the Pinkerton Agency," explained Johnny.

"How long have you been developing your conglomerate?" asked Tom.

"Let's see ... Ruth and I were married six years ago, and it started when I opened that sawmill to finish the wood that I needed for our house. I just looked about me and saw all the new people coming into the area, and the new cities springing up and put two and two together, and things grew faster than my wildest dreams. I recognized God's hand in everything that I did and gave to the Mission and to a church in Amarillo where I attend. God did the rest, I guess."

"Amazing. Just amazing!" said Tom.

"I know where you can get a bank manager. That's what I do in Houston now, and if you would be willing to match my income, I'll come to work for you. Sounds like your banks are growing," spoke up Cheryl.

"Well, I didn't know what work you did, but I would be thrilled to have you the head of the Ragan Bank of Texas. That would be a big lift for me. We can work out the salary, and you can stay at either of my hotels while you get an apartment. I own three apartments also and have no idea what is vacant."

Melody stood stunned, and Tom didn't know what to say. This was the boy that he thought would never be any more than a cowboy, and Johnny just hired his daughter to go to work for him.

Dinner was served in the dining room, and the cook fixed several of his better dishes. Johnny bragged on the meal, which really pleased the cook.

"I bet you have some good cooks and restaurants too," said Melody.

"I have a private French cook, and I do a lot of entertaining. Business is business, you know, and there are times that I have to impress someone. Pierre, my cook, is a polished gourmet cook. Pierre's wife is Marie, my maid, and they live in an apartment adjacent to mine. Her dad, Woodrow, drives my carriage and grooms my Appaloosa.

"I've bought a nice lot on a hill overlooking the town and have one of my construction companies building a home with attached servant quarters. Pierre and his wife have a lot of input into what they would like in their quarters. I really want them to be happy, for I rely on them completely. Cheryl, maybe when you get settled in your new job you can give me a few pointers for the house I'm building."

"I can hardly wait," said Cheryl. She smiled at her parents.

That evening, George came to the parlor, and Johnny joined him as they sang both the old songs and some new songs that had become popular.

After a while, Tom and Melody excused themselves, and George went to the bunkhouse.

Cheryl sat in a chair and kicked off her shoes. She wanted to know something about the new job and had many questions for her new boss. He found that she was well versed in banking and told her to take charge of the bank and install the most recent ways of accounting. He smiled as he told her that she would need to teach him the new method also. If the new methods worked, he wanted it in all his banks. She may well find herself as a district manager, or a vice-president of banking.

She took his hand and led him to his bedroom, and then turning, she kissed him on the lips.

He pushed the door open and left her standing in the hall, expecting a kiss in return. When the door was shut he thought of Ruth and knew he still loved the Indian girl. Yet it had been a good evening. Tomorrow he needed to get back to his many enterprises. He would make a place for Cheryl, as he really needed someone in banking whom he could trust. Now that she would be near him continually, would things return to the same feelings they had when he gave her the first kiss that she had from a boy?

His thoughts turned to Ruth and the lovely girl he had married. His oath to her had been, "till death do us part," but they were divorced now. His thoughts centered around her health and the reason for the divorce. He slept fitfully as he remembered Cheryl's kiss and thought of Ruth and the extra weight she carried. He dreamed of a girl over a hundred pounds overweight and awoke in a strange room to someone calling his name. Beads of perspiration were on his brow, and Cheryl was calling that breakfast was about ready. He got up and took a sponge bath, shaved, and entered the dining area all refreshed and ready for travel.

Tom, Melody, Cheryl, Howard, and Katherine were all awaiting him. Howard was a lanky teenager, and his sister, Katherine, was a year older and the very image of Cheryl.

Tom introduced Johnny to his two teenage children. "I guess you're all packed up and ready to go. Cheryl will need to give a notice at her bank."

"Tom, I've been thinking about Slim Wilkins, and with your permission I would like to offer him a job working for me as a bodyguard. I need someone I can trust who will watch my back," said Johnny.

"Slim's a good man, and I owe him my life, for he killed a carpetbagger, Robbie, when I couldn't pull the trigger in a gun fight," stated Tom.

Breakfast was soon over, and Katherine came to Johnny and kissed him on the cheek. "I'm very happy to know you." Howard stood and shook Johnny's hand. Johnny rode out to where the TM cowboys were branding steers. They all gathered around him and shook his hand. George was a foreman of the crew, and Johnny called Slim to one side.

"Slim, I talked with Tom, and he granted me permission to talk to you. I need a bodyguard, someone who will watch my back. I'll pay you a $125.00 a month and room and board if you'll consider the job."

Slim looked at Johnny and studied him for a minute. "It's true, then, what I've heard, that you've hit the jackpot! Johnny, it couldn't have happened to a more deserving guy. Since it's all right with Tom, I'll look forward to helping you. When do you want me to start?"

"Right now. Tom said that you didn't need to give him a notice. There's no one who could replace you anyway." Slim grinned when he heard that.

"I'll get my gear and be with you in about fifteen minutes. I want to stop by the hacienda and say good-bye." He turned to the working crew, told them he was leaving, and they all gathered around and wished him the best. Slim stopped at the hacienda and hugged Melody and said good-bye to Howard and Katherine and started to do the same to Cheryl when she told him that she was going too.

"Watch out for Cheryl, Slim, there are a lot of bank robbers out there, and times are hard," said Tom.

"See you." Cheryl grinned. Johnny and Slim rode North and looked up the home of Rex and Erma. Rex was surprised to see them, and Erma kissed both men.

"Rex, the cattle trails are about the thing of the past, and you'll soon be out of a job," began Johnny. "The railroad is here to stay!"

"Aw, you don't need to rub it in," drawled Rex.

"Rex, I need a lot of help, and I've several places where I could use you and your expertise. Amos is helping with the mills, and I need someone who will manage my hauling business. Erma, if you want to work, I need someone to help manage my mercantile stores."

"When do we start?"

"I'll meet you at nine o'clock at our depot. Do you know where it is?" Johnny asked.

"Everyone in Amarillo knows where it is," said Rex.

"With all the robbery that's going on, you might not get much sleep for a while. Some of the robbery is inside my business, and Rex, you'll need to be very careful. Slim and I will try to gather some trustworthy men who can back you. You and Slim are those I can trust," added Johnny. "Erma, if you decide to work, try to come with Rex. There are some Indian ladies who are good Christians who will work for you. I'll pay the help for you. Your children will be well cared for. Schools are getting better in Amarillo. Your home in the city has a lot of possibilities for commercial property."

Johnny and Slim rode on into Amarillo, and Johnny pointed out several buildings that he owned. "That's the Ragan Building where I work, and it's mostly office buildings. Near the railroad station is the Ragan Transport and Freight Building, where Rex will have his office. Slim, I want you to check in with him every day, as a lot of my problems come out of the freight portion of my business. I want for us to help him all we can.

"There's my main mercantile store, but there are three more in town that are run from this store. Erma will have her office in there if she decides to come on board. I've been having trouble balancing my books among the stores too. I also have three banks in town, and Cheryl will be running them.

"With your help, I look forward to getting in the black again. I tell you, they tried to rob me blind! I feel that there is a continuity in their stealing. I must find the people who are doing this to me. When our group all get in place, I want a meeting of you all each week until we solve some of the mystery of this stealing. There's a lot of money involved, and they won't go down easily. Slim, you'll need to really be on your toes, and don't trust anyone except our inner group. They have killed before and will do so again, I feel," said Johnny.

"Tell me about the killing," said Slim.

"I hired a Pinkerton detective from the railroad to work under-cover. You know that I own most of the railroad that comes in here. Anyway, he had his suspicion regarding a group of mule skinners who carried freight from the railroad to various designations. The paperwork was backing his suspicions, and he told me that he was about to make an arrest. We found him with a knife in his back, lying near the railroad tracks. I have another Pinkerton detective working undercover who will work closely with Rex and you. His name is Samuel Mahoney. Yep, he is one hundred percent Irish and a good man! I want you and Rex to meet him, but we must be careful not to blow his cover. He'll slip into my office by the back way, which I'll show you. I have six keys that will fit the door, and he has one of them. Rex, Cheryl, Samuel, you, and I will have keys, and Erma will have one if she comes on board. When I want him to report to me, I pull the window blind on my front window down all the way and give him a day to see it.

He goes to work along this street every day, and all he needs to do is look up here and then come just after dark. I wait for him until he's here. This back stairs are not used by anyone but me.

"Slim, let's go over to my place on Amarillo Blvd., where they're building my home. You'll have a room there and enjoy the cooking of Pierre. The house is complete on the outside, and we have used some of the yellow brick from my own brickyards. You can sure see it a good distance, but the brick is glazed, and with white mortar makes an attractive house. You can either ride in the surrey with me or use your own horse. I've five really good horses in the stable behind the dwelling, but leave me my horse, the Appaloosa, Jack, as he doesn't let anyone on him but me. I'd hate to see you with a broken leg your first week."

"Me too!" Slim grinned.

The house was completed on the outside, with much of the interior in place. There were a lot of plastered walls drying and waiting to be painted. The massive, curved stairs leading to the second floor were made of walnut and expertly carved. Floors were being laid where the plaster had set up. Both men went to the second floor, where Slim claimed a bedroom just at the top of the stairs. Anybody climbing the stairs would need to pass his bedroom before reaching the master bedroom down the hall.

Voices attracted their attention where Pierre, Marie, and Woodrow were in conversation downstairs in their quarters. Johnny led Slim to their door, and his knock brought all three to the door. Pierre was thin and dark-complexioned and had black hair with a moving Adam's apple. He wore an apron and had a small mustache. Marie was petite and had black hair and wore a black maid's uniform. She proved to be jovial and had a French accent, as did Pierre. Woodrow was a big man and wore a uniform and a top hat. He, too, was jovial. Johnny introduced them to Slim and told them what his job was. Slim would be head of security, and they needed to work with him if they saw anything unusual.

They all shook hands.

"We won't be eating here tonight, Pierre, but is the kitchen to your liking? You order all the cooking utensils that you need, and I'll have them delivered. The painters will be here tomorrow to put the second coat on the downstairs and finish the kitchen area. Day after tomorrow I want a six o'clock breakfast and six o'clock evening meals. Slim will be eating with us.

"Woodrow, I'll be riding the Appaloosa the next couple of days. Watch him when you saddle him, as he may bite you. He doesn't like anyone but me, and no one will ride him but me," said Johnny.

Cheryl was requested to give a week's notice, so she telegraphed Johnny that she would be there on a Monday morning, April 4, 1891.

Johnny contacted Woodrow, who brought the coach, and Johnny and Slim met her as her train came in from Houston. Rex walked over from his office and joined Johnny and Slim as they waited while the train came to a stop.

Cheryl, dressed in a blue dress and bustle, was helped by the porter down the steps. All three men admired her beauty and poise. The blue dress made her blue eyes look large. People turned and admired her as she walked toward the waiting men.

"Hello, Cheryl! My, but don't you look beautiful," said Rex, and Johnny and Slim all agreed. Woodrow was busy carrying luggage to the coach.

Rex and Slim saw all her luggage and ran to help Woodrow. Her face was flushed with happiness, and she brushed Johnny's cheek with a kiss.

"Well, here I am! The train is only half an hour late. Sorry! That train is dirty, full of soot and vulgar men. Slim, shoot that one right there." She pointed to a small man in a brown suit. A gun appeared in Slim's hand, and the man who had heard her make the remark turned white and looked down Slim's gun barrel.

"Shall I shoot him in the leg or in the gizzard?" drawled Slim.

"We'll let him go this time." Slim put his gun away but didn't take his eye off the man, who hurried away and was lost in a laughing crowd.

With the coach loaded down, Rex went back to his office, which was near, and Woodrow drove the coach down to the Ragan Apartments, where Cheryl would live. The apartment was just a half block from The Ragan Bank of Texas, which was the largest bank of the four owned by Johnny.

Johnny had four men waiting to carry Cheryl's luggage to her apartment. Woodrow stayed with the coach, and Johnny and Slim escorted Cheryl to her apartment. It was a five-room apartment with a balcony that looked out onto the city. Cheryl was delighted and beamed with happiness as Johnny pointed out the bank where she would work. The brick building had large glass doors and four marble columns at the front.

"Your office will be in that bank building. On the first Monday of the month our inner group will meet at my office building, and you will come up the back stairs. I'll give you a key for the back door to my office. Slim will be the security officer and will be there to protect you. Always listen to him in matters of security. We'll leave you to unpack. Marie, my maid, is here to help you, and you may use her for a couple of days, and from then on you'll need to get your own maid.

"I'll be back at 5:45 to take you to dinner. Sorry, I own no restaurants but there are a few here that I would recommend. Till 5:45, depend on Marie for what you might need. By the way, you look lovely." He brushed her with a peck on her cheek as he went by.

"He's uncomfortable around you. He's so lonely; I hope that you'll help fill the sadness in his life with happiness. Watching you two, I believe you can do it," said Marie after Johnny was gone. Cheryl looked oddly at Marie then smiled.

"I intend to replace all the sadness in his heart with love and happiness," said Cheryl.

"You've a lot of competition, for every eligible girl in Amarillo would love to do the same. But the way he looked at you, you may be the one," said Marie.

Cheryl got busy unpacking and was thrilled by Marie's words. At 5:45 Johnny was at her door, dressed in a dark brown suit. They dined out at one of the local restaurants, and Cheryl noticed Slim, who watched every person who approached them.

"Are times here that dangerous? Does Slim stay that close to you all the time?" asked Cheryl, alarmed.

"I have my reasons to be careful, and yes, this is a dangerous place. Slim is very careful, and he will be near you. Don't be alarmed, but we're being extra cautious. The Texas Rangers have informed me that there are several robberies that have taken place in this city in the past month. Rex is on to something already in his hauling business. We believe that this group of crooks are led by a shrewd man or woman. The fact that they've already murdered make them even more dangerous. Sorry, but that's the way that it is right now. We aim to clean out the bad and elevate the good. Don't worry your pretty head; we'll watch you closely," explained Johnny.

He put his hand over hers and squeezed her hand. That was the only sign of affection that he demonstrated. He refused her invitation to come into her apartment, but only after a moment of hesitation. He gave her a key to the back stairs of his office and told her he'd pick her up for the inner group meeting at 8:45 in the morning.

Woodrow came to her door and escorted her down to the coach, where Johnny sat reading a paper. He wore a shirt and tie, for it was a spring day, and the weather was clear and beautiful. His office covered the entire fifth floor of the office building. Woodrow pointed out the back stairs and turned as she inserted her key and opened the door into a meeting room. Rex, Slim, Erma, and Amos were there drinking coffee. They all crowded around Cheryl, and the greetings were all enthusiastic and cordial. Johnny held the coffee pot and poured coffee for everyone, pointing to a small table that had sugar and cream.

"Welcome, everyone! I want you to meet Nina, my private secretary, who will take notes at this meeting for us. " He turned to a very pretty blonde girl who wore glasses and had her hair piled on top of her head.

"Nina has been with us for three months and does a good job. She's a special person to me. She is my younger sister. We have been looking for my brother, who is somewhere in Oklahoma." Nina nodded to all as they greeted her to the meeting.

"Also, this is Samuel Mahoney, who is working undercover for us. He is with the Pinkerton Detective Agency, and since his time is limited, I want him to make his report first."

Samuel was short and very muscular. He had a red face and straw-colored hair. It was evident that he was a strong man and could handle himself in any battle.

"I have been working the loss of our ten wagons of merchandise and believe that there are two Kiowa Apache that are responsible. They are both teamsters and were gone for a week after the robbery of the wagons. They claimed they both got away from their captives, who were white rustlers. I hired a tracker who followed the wagons to a Kiowa reservation in Oklahoma. The wagons are setting behind the reservation, in a ravine, but by this time may be destroyed. These two that returned to us are Gray Fox and Laughing Dog. I have noticed that they disappear when Mr. Ragan is around. I could arrest them, but it is up to you all, as we can prove nothing on them."

"Rex, do you have an inventory of what was in those ten wagons, and can the material be recognized?" questioned Johnny. "I wonder if that reservation is the one at the Mission. Red Hand wouldn't stand for the stealing, if his tribe was involved. Rex, try to talk with the trackers and get the exact location. We'll watch these two men and try to catch them in the act of stealing. After we go over the inventory of those ten wagons, let's ship basically the same materials, but let me know and I, with some help, will trail the wagons and try to catch them in the act."

Rex nodded agreement, and Amos indicated he would like to be there to help apprehend the robbers.

"I have all your reports and have gone over each of them. Cheryl hasn't yet been to her office and of course has no report, but Nina Ragan has a report from Norman Foster, who has been acting manager till Cheryl can get started. Here is his report, Cheryl, so look it over, and maybe you can make heads or tails of it. Rex, you haven't been here very long, but you've made out an interesting report," Johnny continued.

"Yes, sir, I show a profit of $3,500 for the month. But we lost that much when we lost those ten wagon loads of merchandise to bandits a week ago. Two of my teamsters were killed when bandits hit us north of here. I'm thrilled regarding the success of Samuel Mahoney. I don't know Gray Fox or Laughing Dog. Johnny, maybe you might know these two, and if we can get you into my office unseen, you can see the men loading wagons from my office. You might be able to identify them," said Rex, and Slim nodded his agreement.

Cheryl put down the report she had been studying. "It appears that there was a profit of $25,000 last month from loans made in Real Estate and in building materials. This is the total from all four banks. I would say that we had a good month. Looks good on paper at least," remarked Cheryl.

Amos stood and turned to his boss and friends. "We're as busy as we can get and have added contracts from the Railroad for treated ties. There are so many new towns springing up that the demand for lumber is almost overwhelming. I've added several Indians to my working crew, and seasoned lumber is more and more in demand. My kilns have been burning night and day in all four of our mills. More and more bricks are being ordered, and we're having trouble keeping up with the demand."

"Sounds good! Nice work, Amos!" praised Johnny.

"The railroads are just about out of our area, but right of way is being purchased to connect with other major towns toward our south. I see another five years or so and maybe longer in which the railroad will need our services," remarked Johnny.

Erma, who had decided to join Johnny with her husband, made her report of the mercantile stores, and the profit was $2,500, which wasn't bad at all. She said that it was all new and she needed some help with the bookkeeping portion of the work. Cheryl said she would assist her.

Johnny was well pleased with the work of the circle of friends and the way they had all pitched in. "My house will be completed before the month is out, and I want you all to come to a party that I'll be giving. I'm hoping that William will be taking a job with me in the near future. I have these three construction companies I want him to run. Of course, he is in the army now, and we need him to go with us to the Mission field when we try to root out the source of all this stealing."

Johnny adjourned the meeting with a prayer, and all were pleased with the progress of the company.

The next morning early Johnny went up the back stairs to Rex's office and sat in the dark until Rex came in. Samuel Mahoney came into the office shortly after, and they all sat in the dark and waited for the teamsters to arrive and begin loading wagons from several railroad cars. There were several Kiowa Indians that carried out materials from the railroad boxes.

"Johnny, Rex, see these next two teamsters. The first one is Laughing Dog and the next one is Gray Fox," said Samuel Mahoney.

"I know them, or maybe I have seen them before, but where?" remarked Johnny. "Now I remember! It was at the reservation when I made a purchase; they followed me and tried to rob me. I fought them and was knifed. Red Hand turned them over to the military, I believe. I didn't have to testify against them for some reason. I hit Gray Fox in the head with my hob-nailed boots. I was told that they were not of Red Hand's tribe but were Kiowa Apache. They have to be tied in with someone around that reservation. There was a young lieutenant, and then there was William Schmitt, the commissioner. You don't think he had anything to do with it, do you? It would be a good outlet to sell my goods to the army or to the Kiowa reservation. Well, I'll be! You know he saw my money when I bought a few items that I needed. Why, that sneaking renegade! It all makes sense, but maybe we had better try to catch him with the goods."

Rex picked up the invoice and read where the shipment was going.

"It's going to the reservation! Do you think they might fake a robbery and deliver these to the commissioner? There are to be four wagons of supplies; Samuel Mahoney is down there checking the wagons and will have the drivers sign the inventory as a receipt. I wonder if the other two drivers are in on this too?"

"Rex, Amos, Slim, Samuel Mahoney, and I will not let those wagons out of our sight, so we'd all better head for a good night's sleep and let Rex go in by himself in the morning and check them out as usual. When they have gone, Rex light out up here toward my office, and we'll follow them. Any questions?"

•

A pale orange could be seen in the east as Amos, Slim, Samuel, and Johnny mounted their horses in front of the Ragan Office Building. No one spoke, for in the cool of the early morning, sound traveled well. They just nodded a morning greeting to one another.

A town Marshall rode up to Johnny and nodded to him as Johnny turned his Appaloosa toward the railroad. Rex came down the street riding his horse, and all spoke a good morning to him.

"They're all loaded and on the trail and will need to cross the Canadian. They should have little difficulty, but they'll take their time in doing it," explained Rex. "If it's all right, I'll follow them closely and let you all know when they've crossed the river. One fellow will be more difficult to see than the dust of five of us."

"Good idea! We'll hold back till they have crossed the river and watch from a distance," said Johnny.

Rex rode off at a cantor, and the rest sat for a while to give him some lead time. The eastern sky was turning from pink to orange when all rode after Rex. By the time they reached where they could make out Rex, the teams were all across the river. Rex waved to them, and they all proceeded to cross the river. They turned more west and rode, watching for Rex, who was scouting ahead of them. Just about mid-afternoon they overheard the sounds of gunfire and moved forward with uncertainty. Rex rode to meet them.

"A group of Apache has attacked the wagons and killed the two extra drivers." said Rex.

"You can't take the blame for that, Rex. I thought they were into the thing with Laughing Dog and Gray Fox too. How many Apache were in the attack?" asked Johnny.

"I saw four, but Laughing Dog shot the teamsters in the back. The dirty, murdering renegade! Two of the attackers are driving the teams, and that leaves two Apache who will be watching the back trail," said Rex.

"Amos, you know where this trail leads, but is there another route that can take us to the Mission without being seen? Rex, you and Slim follow the teams, and Samuel and I will follow Amos. We'll make a whole lot less dust, and we can get ahead of them," said Johnny. "Rex, Slim, be careful not to be seen and don't crowd them. I'm almost sure they are headed toward the reservation."

It was dark when Johnny, Amos, and Samuel got back to the trail. Approximately a mile away they could see the campfire of the teamsters and Indians.

"I brought along some jerky, and there are some biscuits and bacon and a couple cans of beans and peaches. Looks like a cold meal, but what I have will keep us from starving," said Johnny. "I'll take the first watch just in case there are some other Apache in the area. Slim, I'll wake you at midnight, and then Samuel will spell you at three o'clock. A small fire for coffee at dawn wouldn't hurt." Johnny took his Winchester and settled down among some rocks, where he could see the surrounding territory. He was very alert.

Johnny awoke to the smell of coffee and frying bacon. Amos had built a small fire, well sheltered, and used dry wood so that there was no smoke. Slim and Amos each had a cup of coffee, and Slim was taking a cold biscuit and sopping some bacon grease, rolling a piece of hot bacon around on his tongue. Amos was grinning at Slim, who was trying his best not to get burnt. Johnny stood watching and thinking what great friends these two men had turned out to be, and, reaching down with his biscuit, he repeated the actions of Slim.

"Coffee?" asked Amos and handed Johnny a steaming hot cup. Samuel came down from the rocks and poured a cup of coffee and went to the frying pan for his bacon. When the men finished eating, what was left in the coffee pot was poured on the fire, and dirt was kicked over the coals. Horses were saddled and led to water, and the four started their day believing that before the day was over there would be an arrest made. Johnny stood among the men and in the light of the new day drew a diagram of the reservation.

"It's my opinion that those teams will ride right up to the commissioner's building as if this were ordered material about to be delivered. Amos, I want you to ride to Red Hand and tell him the full story. Have Red Hand contact the lieutenant, and Amos, I want him there when I make the accusation. I think that William Schmitt will give up without a fight, but Laughing Dog and Gray Fox are murderers. I want Red Hand to watch them. Watch those Apache. Samuel, you and the lieutenant will need to make the arrest."

Amos and Slim rode for the Reservation while Samuel and Johnny watched for the wagons. The day was about spent when Johnny and Samuel heard the rumbling of the wagons as they approached the reservation. The whole reservation was quiet, and Johnny hoped Red Hand and the military officers were in place. He didn't hear a thing except the approaching wagons. The back door to the commissioner's office was ajar, and Johnny could see William Schmitt standing for a second in the doorway before he exited the building. The wagons all came to a stop adjacent to the commissioner's building, and there was some talk made in the Apache tongue.

"Good job, men! This, with the other ten wagons, will bring a handsome income for us," spoke William Schmitt. "Did we lose anyone?"

A voice rang out in a sharp tone. "Put 'em up! You're all under arrest." It was the voice of the lieutenant. There was a rapid fire that exploded from around the area. The Apache were resisting, and the military had opened fire. The Winchester fire that was added to the battle came from Rex and Slim. The military had been told they would be near. The battle was over quickly, and six Apache lay on the ground, among them were Gray Fox and Laughing Dog. William Schmitt was cursing that he'd been caught. Several had heard the remark that he'd made regarding the stolen ten wagons. A huge first sergeant tied him and took him, bound, to the guard house at the military post.

"Nice work, fellows," said Johnny. Crowds of military and Indians flooded the area. John Beasley, Causes to Laugh, and Ruth were at the front of the Mission asking questions and were dismayed that William Schmitt had been involved.

Johnny was taken to the adjutants' office, where he filed a complaint against William Schmitt and showed the evidence that he had and the inventory of the stolen goods. Johnny was told that he might be called to testify at the trial. Since it was on the reservation, it would be a military trial. The total goods would be restored, including the ten wagonloads of the prior robbery. Amos, Rex, Slim, and Samuel Mahoney were guests of the U.S. Army, and Johnny said he would spend the night at the Mission.

Johnny rode his Appaloosa to the Mission corral, where he fed the horse and put him in the stable for the night.

Johnny went to the Mission and rapped gently on the door. Causes to Laugh came with an oil lamp and held it high to make sure of the identity of Johnny. She turned, set the lamp down, and then ran into Johnny's arms. John was behind her and saw who it was and put his arms around the both of them.

"Welcome, son! Welcome!" said John. Causes to Laugh was shedding large tears of joy.

"What's all the commotion?" asked Ruth, as she walked into the room and stood very still as all three turned to her. Ruth had lost some weight, and it was no secret that she was just fine again. She didn't know whether to laugh or cry. A large tear came from her right eye and ran down across her smiling face.

"Hi, Johnny!" He reached for her, but she was hesitant. He crushed her in his arms, but she stiffened and drew back. John Beasley and Causes to Laugh were watching Ruth and Johnny closely. He tried to kiss her, but she turned her head, whereon Johnny released her and stepped back.

"I'm sorry, Johnny, but it's too soon. I need to heal some more. I'm glad to see you, which shows a lot of improvement." Another tear rolled down her cheek.

"Thank you," spoke Johnny and backed away from Ruth. He would give her a lot of time. She looked better than she had for six months, and being with her folks must be a great part of the cure.

"We were just starting to sit down for supper; please come and join us, as there is plenty of food," said Causes to Laugh. John stepped forward, took Johnny's hands, and they went into the dining room together. Causes to Laugh stood looking at her daughter.

"Honey, he still loves you, so be nice to him. He won't try to kiss you again; he's a good man and will wait for you if you still love him."

"Mother, I'm still all mixed up, but he's the only man that I will ever marry," said Ruth.

Together they sat down as a family, and Johnny broke bread with them. John and Causes to Laugh did more talking than usual, but there was a strain between Ruth and Johnny.

"Tell me about this robbery attempt," said John. Johnny told him of losing the ten wagon loads of merchandise and then the setting of the trap with the four wagons that led to the killing of the six Apache and arresting of William Schmitt. Johnny told of his need for help and how Slim, Amos, Rex, Erma, and Cheryl had been hired to help him. When Cheryl's name was mentioned, Ruth took special notice and sat up stiffly in her chair.

"How are they helping you?" asked John, who had noticed the change in Ruth.

"Amos is in charge of the lumber mills and brick quarry. Rex is in charge of hauling and the railroad yards, Erma is in charge of the mercantile stores, and Cheryl is the head of my banking system. Slim is in charge of security. There is another person you need to meet. Her name is Nina Ragan. She is—" Johnny was interrupted by a scream from Ruth.

"Oh Johnny, how could you? I didn't think you would marry anyone other than me." She leaped from the table and ran weeping toward her room.

"Wait, Ruth, wait!" called Johnny, but Ruth was gone.

"Nina is my sister! Causes to Laugh, please hurry and tell her! I've found my lost sister and am looking for my little brother. Nina is my secretary." Causes to Laugh hurriedly left the room as John smiled.

"That's one way of finding out her true thought, Johnny. She truly still loves you dearly. She will feel foolish for a while, but the shock should help her. She got a taste of what it would be if you really found another," said John. "We would like for you to stay with us tonight, and just maybe you can see Ruth in the morning. There's no way that she will face you this evening."

"I agree! John, I wouldn't have mentioned Nina if I thought it would have the effect that it did. I thought finding Nina would be a joy to Ruth. I guess you want me in my old room. I have a check for you and the Mission, and I might as well give it to you now." Johnny turned the check over to John.

"There's something else I wanted to tell Ruth. I'm building a home in Amarillo, and it should be finished by the time that I get back. I have a full-time cook, maid, and I will ask Nina to share my home with me. Slim, my bodyguard, has a room there, as does Woodrow, my horseman. The Lord is really blessing me, and

I appreciate it," said Johnny. "I'm hoping that William, Cheryl's twin, will be getting out of the army soon, and can take charge of the three construction companies. William majored in engineering at Virginia Military Institute and would be an excellent help in that field. He should be getting out any time now."

"Ruth got your check from the sale of your old house and was very sad for a few days. Your monthly check has been more than she needs, but she is saving her money and gives to the Mission as well as looks for some way to help among the tribal people." Causes to Laugh came back with tears in her eyes but a smile on her face.

"Ruth will be all right. She felt terribly foolish when I told her Nina was your sister you had found. She said that she feared you would find someone, yet she wanted you to find happiness. She is still a very mixed-up young lady, and I'm not so sure she will want to see you in the morning, but she did say that she was so very glad you found your sister."

John told Causes to Laugh Johnny would be staying the night, and so Causes to Laugh led Johnny to his old bedroom and fixed the bed for him. As she worked, Johnny told her of his new house going up and of his servants.

The next morning, Johnny heard Causes to Laugh singing a hymn as she prepared breakfast. He arose and had devotions with John Beasley, but Ruth didn't make an appearance. He ate breakfast, thanked his former mother-in-law, and then walked into the Indian camp, where he visited with Red Hand and Red Doe. He walked on into the army camp and found his crew ready to leave. He thanked the army officials, especially the young lieutenant, for their assistance. He stopped by the Mission, saddled the Appaloosa, and waved to Causes to Laugh and John Beasley but still saw no sign of Ruth.

WILLIAM MCDOWELL JOINS JOHNNY'S TEAM

Johnny led his crew back into Amarillo, and as news spread of the arrest of William Schmitt, Johnny got an unexpected visitor. William McDowell rode into Amarillo and walked into Johnny's office.

"Hello, Johnny! Well, I'm no longer in the U.S. Army; got my discharge last week and have been riding toward home. Cheryl has been writing to me of your success in business and that you have need for an engineer to work in your construction companies."

"Man, am I glad to see you, William, I've more work than I can possibly do and have several houses under construction, but I need someone like William McDowell to oversee the entire construction business. I was planning to write to you and offer you the job. Interested? You sure look good, and I believe that being a soldier has been good for you," stated Johnny.

"How is sis? I haven't been to see her yet."

"I think she will move things around so she can work you in. She has some very good ideas and really has changed banking in Amarillo. She's been trying to make me understand her ways of bookkeeping. We've stopped losing money and have fired a couple that might have had their hand in the till. She's not only a beautiful, refined lady, but smart too," stated Johnny.

"Heard that your wife divorced you, Johnny... I was sorry to hear that, but Cheryl still loves you, you know," remarked William.

"We work some long hours together, but that's all that it has been, just work. She, Nina, and I have been working hard."

"Who is Nina?"

Johnny walked to the door and called into the outer office, where Nina worked.

"Nina, come in here a minute!"

Blond-headed, blue-eyed Nina came in with her pad. William immediately showed interest.

"William, this is my little sister, Nina Ragan. She is not only my sister but my secretary and a mighty sweet young lady." Johnny smiled. "Nina, this is Cheryl's twin brother, and my friend. I taught him everything that he knows except engineering. This is William McDowell."

They stood looking at each other for a full minute, and then Nina blushed a deep red. Johnny saw the interest that they had in one another, and it made him extremely happy.

"How do you do?" asked William, and he bowed to her and took her hand in his. He was a perfect gentleman, and Nina recognized his college training and military background.

"I'm fine, thank you!" She looked to her older brother to help her out, for she was at a loss as to what to say to this handsome young man.

"William may come to work for me, and if he does, he'll be the head of the construction companies. Nina, at the party at the house tonight I want you to introduce him to everyone. Cheryl may want to help you to see that everyone meets her brother. Dinner will be served at six o'clock," said Johnny.

"May I pick you up and see that you get there all right?" asked William.

"I live there now," said Nina. "But I will take you around and introduce you to our guests."

"Great!" William smiled as Nina returned to her work.

"Wow, Johnny, I'm in love! Did she ever put me into the Ragan conglomerate! Shall I work for free just to be around her? Where did she get her blond hair when you have black? She has the bluest eyes I've ever seen, except maybe my mother's and Cheryl's."

"My mother was a blonde, and Dad had black hair so I guess that's how it happened. My brother also had dark hair when I saw him last," explained Johnny. "William, it's settled, then? You will be in charge of the three construction companies? I'll take you in as a partner in that part of my business, if you wish, or you can work at a salary. We'll work something out!

You'd better get over to the bank and see Cheryl; I'll take you over if you wish. Come on over here to this window—that's the bank where her office is and the largest building in town. She's on the top floor. You may have to wait to see her ... Ha! She is a darling!" Johnny smiled.

"I'll slip in and surprise her! I'm looking forward to dinner tonight. It's informal, isn't it?" asked William.

"Yes, informal. Good to have you on board, William." Johnny shook Williams's hand.

That evening Johnny, Nina, Rex, Erma, Amos, and Red Doe greeted people as they arrived. Rex and Amos were uncomfortable in broadcloth suits but had string ties and Texas boots. Amos was uncomfortable in boots, for he usually wore moccasins. Johnny and Nina greeted the mayor of the town and his wife, as well as the sheriff and his wife. The captain of the local Texas rangers and his wife were there also. William came in with Cheryl on his arm.

She was dressed in a light blue gown, which caused her eyes to look even bluer. Her light brown hair had a blue ribbon in it, and her garment was the latest fashion; she smiled as she looked at Johnny. He kissed her lightly on the cheek and whispered to her how lovely she looked.

"Why don't you ever tell me that when we are alone at work?" She smiled. Nina was the only one that heard her remark, but her attention was turned to William, who was in a blue broadcloth suit and very handsome. Nina had on a light green dress, and the garment was the latest style from New York. She wore a blouse that overlapped the low cut dress and showed a lot of taste, and her conservative thoughts on dress.

Marie, the maid, served some punch while Johnny took his guests through his new house, pointing out various highlights. He had spared no expense in the construction of the house, for one day he would share it with a wife and children. But for Ruth or Cheryl? He walked through each room explaining this and that, when he noticed all the input that Cheryl had made to the building. The drapes and the color scheme were her ideas—the chandeliers, dishes, and the silverware were her selections. If Ruth knew this, would she approve? Had he not asked Ruth for her decisions relative to various items? Yes, and she turned from the idea with anger.

Suddenly, Johnny and Cheryl were in the upstairs hall. He turned her toward him and gave her a passionate kiss. Cheryl responded with enthusiasm, and then he held her at arm's length. She wanted more, but there was movement at the end of the hall, and guests were coming up the steps.

His heart ached. He owed nothing to Ruth now—had she not divorced him? Wasn't her reason for the divorce to allow him to find another? She didn't want a child for fear of losing it in a miscarriage. Could he ever have a marriage relationship with Ruth again? And yet, when he saw her last at the Mission, she looked so much improved.

Cheryl pulled Johnny into the master bedroom, out of the hallway, and out of sight of visitors. She came again into his arms. Her kisses enflamed him, and he had feelings of desire, which he knew belonged only to married people. He tore himself away from her and led her out of his bedroom and back into the hall.

"Let us get our guests back into the dining area, as Pierre has prepared such a fine meal."

He walked in a daze for a few minutes, and his knees were wobbly, but he had conquered the moment.

Nina was the object of William's thoughts, and she showed interest in him. He was a perfect gentleman, which Nina was not used to. Nina was a delightful person and living a good, Christian life. The uncle that raised her had died just a month before she'd found her brother. She was wondering where she could get a job. Her younger brother had seen Johnny's name on wagons used for hauling products and the name Ragan's Hauling written on the side and knew that the name was not a common one. She used the last of her money for the train ride into Amarillo and applied for a job, and when Johnny saw the name on the application, he had rushed to her, held her a moment at arm's length and asked, "Nina?"

And she answered, "Yes, yes, yes!"

Big brother had found his little sister, and now Nina was living in his new house and had food, clothing, and family.

Johnny had many questions for her. How was Samuel, their little brother? How is our uncle? Did he mistreat you and Sam? Is Sam well?

She answered them one by one. "Samuel left home a year after our uncle had died and worked and cared for me. Uncle failed in health until I was left to care for him. He was good to me in his way, but he was always a hard, strict man. He died, and Sam and I buried him behind his house behind the blacksmith shop."

Men had always paid a lot of attention to her, but her Christian ways had discouraged them. She moved her membership to the First Christian Church of Amarillo, where she found Christian fellowship. Johnny attended the church with her regularly and was a big contributor in song and finances. The church also sponsored the Mission at the reservation, and she found an excellent outlet for her interest in her God. She had a lovely alto voice and sang with Johnny in the church choir.

William took Nina's hand as she stood in the door to say good-bye to the group of special friends who were so dear to her brother.

"I would like to see you again, and I'm sure that I will. Your brother has invited me to head up his three construction companies. At first I was undecided, but there is a very pretty girl named Nina who certainly helped me to make up my mind. Please have dinner with me tomorrow night. I don't know the various restaurants around here, but I'm sure you do. May I pick you up here at seven o'clock?"

Nina stood and watched this young man, and her eyes filled for a moment with tears. "Yes, William, I'd love to go to dinner with you."

William kissed her hand and then said, "Till then!" He bowed and stepped back, and then he was gone. Johnny watched William with Nina, and he smiled as William bowed away.

He was military through and through. Johnny knew William would be the new superintendent of his construction companies.

Rex and Erma were near and said their good nights. Amos and Red Doe were next in line. Samuel Mahoney and his wife had already departed. The major of the town and his wife were with the sheriff and his wife, and they said how lovely the place was and what a great addition it was to the beauty of the city.

Only Cheryl and Slim remained. Johnny turned toward Slim and said, "I want to see that Cheryl gets back to her apartment safely; I won't need you tonight, old friend." Slim grinned and departed.

"After those kisses you gave me, do you think we should take Slim with us?" She grinned. "You might need protection!"

"I'm afraid of myself, Cheryl! I'll behave; well, partially anyway." Cheryl smiled as Johnny approached the surrey. The evening was cool, so she sat close to him as he put a heavy blanket over her legs and tucked her in. He then covered his own legs and clucked to the horse.

Woodrow watched as his boss drove the surrey toward town.

Johnny called, "Woodrow, go on to bed, for I'll not need you anymore tonight. I'll put the horse up myself when I come home," said Johnny. Woodrow nodded and turned toward his apartment over the carriage house.

Cheryl and Johnny rode along for a few minutes.

"Cheryl, you know that I love you," said Johnny. Cheryl looked at him and nodded.

"I love you too, Johnny."

They rode on for a few minutes.

"I made a statement to Ruth that bothers me very much. I promised before God and witnesses that I would keep myself to her and to her only until God separated us by death. Cheryl, Ruth is still living, and even though she divorced me, I'm confused relative to my position in the sight of God," stated Johnny.

"Johnny, Ruth is a very fine girl and doesn't do things harshly. I believe that when she divorced you she was saying that she didn't want you as her husband. She couldn't become a mother, and therefore she didn't want you."

"Yes, that's essentially the very center of her thinking," agreed Johnny.

"What are you supposed to do, then? Live a completely celibate life? She doesn't want it that way but wants you to find another and get married and have children. Don't you agree?" Johnny sat for a full minute, trying to agree with her.

"Do you think Ruth might love me so much that she did this without thought of herself but because she knew that we couldn't cohabit? We could not live normally as man and wife?"

"I don't know, Johnny. I'm too selfish to think, were I in her place, that I could give you up to another. My love for you would require you to cohabit with me." He knew that her face was red, but the meaning was clear. This girl loved him with her whole heart, and the thought of Ruth was very far away. He took her into his arms and kissed her tenderly. It was a very gentle kiss, and she responded to it. Marriage to this girl crept into his mind; he needed to study divorce and remarriage some more, for he didn't want to be out of God's will. People frowned on divorce so much!

They were in front of her apartment building, and he took the weight and strap and attached it to the bridle of the horse. He walked her to her door.

"Would you like to come in?" she asked.

"It's really late, and we both have a lot of work tomorrow." Johnny kissed her good night. As she turned, he heard her mumble something. The meaning was unclear, but it sounded like she said. "I won the battle of Roanoke but lost the battle of Amarillo." She shut the door before he could ask her to explain herself.

•

Johnny was thrilled the way his inner group responded to the load of work that was before them. All phases of his conglomerate were now in focus, and profits soared. Johnny shared his good fortune with all of them. William knew what he was doing, and the construction business greatly matured. William constructed his own house, but it wasn't nearly as fine as Johnny's.

Nina went over almost every day after work and helped him to plan the structure. William joined with her at church, and although he couldn't sing, he sat with his sister as Johnny and Nina sang in the choir.

CAPTAIN GEORGE HANCOCK GETS DEMOTED

Captain George Hancock was an armchair officer and wasn't cut out for military duty, especially in the Oklahoma Territory. On his very first mission, he'd led his detail and followed a band of marauding Indians into what he thought was a box canyon. Instead of the band of Indians being cut off from retreat, he discovered the sides of the canyon were filled with waiting Comanche who fired on his troops and would've destroyed the entire detail had not a second attachment of soldiers overheard the firing and come to his rescue.

In review of the incident, it was found that Captain Hancock had disobeyed a direct order from his commanding officer and brashly followed the Indians into the trap. Captain George Hancock had been court-martialed and would've been forced out of the army were it not for his uncle. The disgrace of the court martial lay heavily on his shoulders, and he began to drink and carouse wherever he could find a saloon. For two years this continued, and he was broken in rank back to a second lieutenant. His uncle disowned him, and his family abandoned him. Finally, he could take soldiering no longer and resigned his commission.

He journeyed south into Texas, where he visited every bar he could find until his money ran out. Half drunk, he sat with his head on his arms and heard the bartender refuse him a rye drink for lack of funds. He'd fallen as low as he thought possible and needed money badly, but how could he earn money in Texas? He was in want for food, and when near a bar, he'd grab popcorn from the bar prior to being beaten and thrown out.

JOE WAYNE BRUMETT

He overheard a group telling of the large bank in Amarillo, Texas. He'd lost a lot of weight, and gone were his integrity and self-esteem. He looked across the bar into the big mirror that hung behind the bar and didn't recognize himself but stared in horror at this strange man staring back at him. His wits were acute due to hunger, and he overheard a group planning the robbing of the Ragan Bank of Amarillo.

"We need two more at least, for that bank is huge, and there may be guards. We need someone to keep them covered while we pillage the money drawers and get into the vault. Have any idea who we can get?" asked one of the outlaws.

"I'd like the job," said George Hancock.

"Who are you?" asked one of the trio. The trio turned their attention on George as he boldly approached them.

"I'm Ryan Snelling. I'm from Kentucky, and I need the job!" lied George. He sat down at their table and looked the part. They began to pump him relative to his ability.

"Can you shoot? Do ya have a record with the law? Are the Texas Rangers tailing ya? Have ya any reputation in bank robbery?"

He answered each question and stretched the truth when it was beneficial to him. One paid for a meal for him, while another bought him a beer. He still wore the trousers of a trooper and told them that he was kicked out of the military because of gambling. This was what they wanted to hear, and they took him into their confidence. He demonstrated that he was an average shot with his rifle, and they decided he'd do well as a look out and for him to back them and watch out for the law.

The plan was very simple: The bank opened at nine in the morning, and three would enter the bank while George kept watch at the door. Another bandit would be outside holding the horses. The money was to be taken about five miles from the bank to a deserted homestead where the loot would be divided, and the gang would split up.

George watched every move each member made, for he didn't trust any of them. His life was at stake, and this was something new to him.

RAGAN BANK OF AMARILLO, ROBBED

The entire band rode into Amarillo together and waited as the front doors of the bank were opened. There were a few towns-people waiting for the doors to open, and they rushed into the interior, knowing where to go to be serviced. Once inside the bank, the three interior robbers drew their pistols and cried,

"This is a stickup! Raise your hands and don't try anything, and no one'll get hurt." George stood at the door and watched the backs of all the townspeople. The robbers were behind the cashier's windows and entered the vault, which was ajar. They had gunny-sacks in which they collected cash and walked among the towns-men and robbed them also.

Cheryl came into the bank from a back door and saw the rob-bery in progress. She quickly exited the building and ran to Slim, who was crossing the rear of the property, talking with Johnny. Both men went into action and ran for the bank, each carrying their Winchesters. Slim went in the back door, and Johnny ran along the bank to a side entrance, which was still locked. He con-tinued to the front of the building and saw the robber holding the horses.

Two robbers had finished collecting money from the vault and came out of the front door holding their gunnysacks. George was still in the bank covering the retreating robbers when Johnny fired on the robbers outside the bank. His first two shots killed two of the robbers, and the robber holding the horses quickly surren-dered, dropped his gun to the ground, and lifted both hands.

Slim, followed by Cheryl, came through the back door, and Slim fired into a robber standing in front of a cashier cage. The bullet caught the man in the middle of his chest, and he fell dead.

George put his gun to the temple of one of the townspeople and stood behind him. He called for Slim to drop his gun, which Slim did. George prodded the man toward Cheryl and exchanged him for Cheryl as a hostage. He put his arm around her and held his gun at her temple. Johnny came into the bank and saw what was happening and dropped his own gun for fear that Cheryl might be harmed. George was surprised to see that his hostage was Cheryl, but his beard and long hair was a good disguise, and Cheryl didn't recognize him. He prodded Cheryl out the front door, picked up the three gunnysacks of money, and motioned for her to mount, which she did. George shot the robber who had been holding the horses and rode out of town leading Cheryl's horse.

Johnny rode down to the railroad, where he called for Rex to get together a posse and to join him in pursuit of the outlaw. Johnny couldn't determine which horse was Cheryl's and which was the robber's, as several riders had come into town and the road was covered with horse tracks. Outside the town about three miles, Johnny plainly made out the hoof prints of the two horses that he was following. The robber wasn't trying to cover his tracks, and Johnny pressed them. About two hours later, Johnny dismounted from his Appaloosa and walked him to cool him and rest him. The horse was blowing, and he knew that the horses of Cheryl and the robber were in worse shape than his.

As he walked along, he was thinking of the trail he knew well. It formed a large loop and would turn west. Could he leave the trail and cut though open country and get ahead of them? It would be a challenge, but it was worth the effort. He must continue to press them, for he didn't want the robber to believe he was safe and stop and do harm to Cheryl. Johnny left the trail and rode through wild country until finally he was back on the trail again. He studied the trail and found no tracks, which indicated that he was ahead of them!

He looked on up the trail for possible cover so that he could lay a trap for the robber. He rode to a group of rocks and hid his horse in a clump of trees. He went back and, with a small tree limb, he erased his horse prints from the trail and settled down and waited.

•

"Cheryl, let's walk and cool off our horses," requested George.

She was very surprised. "Do you know me?"

"Yes." As she dismounted, she peered carefully into his eyes; he reminded her of someone, but who? There was the way that he carried his head, was it the blue of his eyes? The black hair? She wouldn't know anyone as dirty and as filthy as this man who smelled of liquor and body odor. Suddenly he reached for her, and she fought him, scratched his face, and he slapped her very hard. The blow nearly knocked her off her feet, whereas he grabbed her hair and held her and forced her to look at him closely.

"Look closely, Cheryl!" She spit into his face. "We've fought before! You slapped me in Roanoke, Virginia," he said.

"George?" She said in amazement and drew back from him, and her eyes studied this filthy, smelly, unclean person. "It is you!"

"Yes, it is I. You kissed me with a lot of feeling at one time in our lives. Can you kiss me now?" His bearded face approached hers, and she struggled to get free from his embrace. She hit him with all her strength and then lunged for her horse. The blow was a surprise to him, and she managed to get to her horse and rode rapidly ahead of him. He gained on her and reached out to grab the reins of her horse. She heard the spat of the bullet as it struck him, and then the gun report. He was lifted off his horse and flung on his back in the trail. She saw Johnny rising out of the rocks, holding his smoking rifle. Johnny held the reins of her horse, while she dismounted, clinging to him. She looked at George lying in the trail.

"Cheryl!" The voice was weak, but it was a plea. "What happened?"

Cheryl looked past Johnny to the dirty bundle lying on the trail. She quickly dismounted and rushed to the dying man. "He knows your name?" inquired Johnny.

"Yes, it's George Hancock. You've never met, but I met him in Virginia while he was a professor at VMI. William had him as a professor and introduced him to me. He was such a handsome man, but oh look at him now."

Cheryl sank down beside George, but his body odor was repugnant. "George, what in the world has happened to you?"

He coughed, and a foamy, bloody bubble came from his mouth; his eyes, full of pain and anger, were fixed on her.

"You've killed me! You, with your uppity ways! I loved you once and wanted you as my wife. Things were so different then. Curses on all the McDowell family. I hate you all!" His cough became a rattle in his chest, for he was drowning in his own blood.

Cheryl drew back from George and hid her face from him.

Johnny moved forward, but George's eyes held anger, and he said, between clenched teeth, "Don't touch me! You've killed me this day, and now you feel sorry for me. I guess you'll want to pray for me next."

"George, I'm sorry that it turned out like this. May the good Lord have mercy on your soul!" These were the last words George heard.

A life wasted by drink, crime, and lost opportunity. Down the trail came the posse, and all dismounted around the robber. The robbery of the bank had been short-lived, and all five of the robbers were dead. George was embalmed and sent by rail back to Virginia. The other four were unknown men who were buried in the cemetery at Amarillo.

WILLIAM MCDOWELL
TAKES A BRIDE

William worked hard at his new job, planning, organizing, and engineering each project. In the evenings he did not fail to forget Nina. The girl, from the day they met, was constantly in his mind. Each day he sought ways to please her. His time at college and his experience in the army had taught him how to respect, love, and cherish women. As the months went by, his interest in her grew until it was difficult to do his engineering without thinking of her.

There came a knock at the back door of Johnny's office, and Slim opened the door. William stood there in his work clothes.

"Slim, may I see Johnny?" asked William.

"I guess you can, ask him." Slim smiled. Johnny was standing right in back of Slim.

"William, come on in!" greeted Johnny. Slim left the office and stepped out where Nina was working in the outer office.

"Johnny, I haven't asked her yet, because I thought I should ask you first; I'd like to ask Nina to be my wife. May I?" asked William.

"William, my sister has her own mind, but nothing would make me happier than for you two to marry," Smiled Johnny. "She's in the next room, and I'll call Slim in here so you can get the job done."

Johnny stood in the doorway and asked Slim to come back into his office. William passed Slim, and Nina was surprised to see him in the middle of the day. Johnny shut the door, and everything got quiet. Johnny could barely hear William's voice and couldn't make out what he was saying, but he could hear Nina.

"Oh yes, William, yes, yes!" Then everything got quiet again. They both opened the door together, and William, smiling, said, "She said 'yes.'"

Johnny hugged his sister and told her that her choice of a man was excellent. William was more than a brother now, he was a brother-in-law to be. Johnny gave them both the day off, and they left to make more plans and to eventually set the date.

About an hour later, there was another knock at the door, and Cheryl came through the outer office all smiles. She hugged Slim, and then Johnny and said that she didn't know a sweeter girl to marry her twin brother than Nina. They had decided to marry as soon as the house was finished, which was estimated to be two weeks away. Johnny told Cheryl that William had proposed in the middle of the day. Cheryl grinned, for William had said, "I was sitting at my desk, and all I could think of was Nina. I was miserable! I couldn't work, had no appetite, I decided I couldn't wait but must act. I just went over to her office right then and asked her to marry me."

"Dad and Mom will be tickled pink, for he'd written them several times about her." Cheryl grinned. Cheryl omitted other remarks made by William in her conversation with Johnny.

"You all planning a big marriage? What kind does Nina want?" Cheryl had asked William.

"We just want a few very special friends; Nina knows our inner group and wants several of Johnny's friends beside. She wants Johnny to give her away and wants you as the maid of honor. But don't tell her that I told you. She wants to ask you personally. Mom and Dad will be there, of course, and I've included all our cowboys. Nina has some friends from the church, she's been writing to John Beasley and his wife, Causes to Laugh, and to Ruth Beasley—she mails a check each month from Johnny."

"Oh no! Do you think Ruth will come? William, do you think she'll invite Ruth?" said Cheryl in alarm. "I think it'll upset Johnny to no end."

"She's already mailed the invitations. Ruth has been corresponding regularly with Nina, and they've gotten to be good friends. Does this alarm you, Cheryl?"

"I'm not sure that it alarms me! It's been many years since I've seen her, but she was Johnny's wife for six years. I heard that she's rather heavy, and her looks may well shame Johnny. He still feels an obligation to her due to the marriage vows he had with her."

"Nina won't renege on her invitation. I won't ask her to," said William.

"Of course not," said Cheryl.

"Nina is upset that she cannot get in touch with her younger brother, Samuel. He is somewhere in Oklahoma where she has written to him but knows the letter could not get to him before the marriage time," added William. "I'm looking forward to meeting Sam too."

Arrangements were made to use the First Christian Church of Amarillo and the minister there to marry them.

Johnny looked over the list of guests and reserved one of his hotels for the cowboys of the TM Ranch and Matt's crew. William invited his old colonel from the army and his wife. Johnny sent letters to John Beasley, Causes to Laugh, and Ruth, Red Hand, and his wife as well, and Amos and his wife, Matt and Bess, that he wanted them to stay overnight at his house. Rex and Erma lived in Amarillo. Tom and Melody McDowell were special guests of William and Nina, who wanted them to stay at their new home. Johnny offered William and Nina his coach or two complimentary railroad tickets to wherever they wanted to go. William and Nina made their plans secretly but agreed to use Johnny's coach.

The day before the wedding, guests were arriving. Cheryl was off for the two days and was helping Marie prepare the various bedrooms at Johnny's house. Erma was there also, cleaning and helping Pierre figure the menu for the quests. Nina was working at her new home, preparing for William's family.

A surrey pulled up in front of Johnny's home, and John Beasley, Causes to Laugh, Red Hand, his wife, and Ruth got out of the surrey with their luggage, while Woodrow tended to the horses and the surrey. They all stood in wonder, gazing at the massive splendor of the yellow brick home of Johnny Ragan.

"Man, isn't that something!" said John. "I hope my mansion in heaven is as nice."

"Absolutely lovely," spoke Causes to Laugh.

"Ugh!" said Red Hand and spoke approving words to his wife in the Kiowa language. "heap big wigwam!"

Ruth looked very beautiful as she admired the house. Erma, Cheryl, and Marie came to the door, and Cheryl had on a maid's apron, and Ruth was dusty from the long trip. They stood staring at each other for a few minutes. The dust of the road could not cover up the extreme beauty of Ruth—her auburn hair was piled high on her head, and her brown eyes had a sparkle in them. Ruth extended her hand to Erma and then to Cheryl.

Erma, Cheryl, and Marie led Johnny's guests to their rooms, and bathtubs were prepared for bathing.

Johnny arrived from his office and apologized for being tardy when they arrived. Pierre prepared an excellent lunch, and they all sat down to eat together; Matt and Bess had arrived earlier, and they sat around the table after the luncheon and talked and drank coffee. Johnny sat looking at both Cheryl and then at Ruth. Ruth was herself again, both girls were very lovely, and Johnny was happy that Ruth appeared to be well now. Cheryl also had the excellent looks of her mother, Melody. Both girls acted as if he wasn't there but talked to one another and showed kindness.

After the meal, Johnny hugged Ruth and told her how fine she looked. He also hugged Causes to Laugh, and they both told him how beautiful his new home was.

"Are you married yet, Johnny? Cheryl is a very sweet girl, and I can see that she loves you very much," asked Causes to Laugh. Ruth overheard her question; her lovely brown eyes were questioning Johnny also.

"No, I, uh, haven't asked anyone to marry me." He looked directly at Ruth. "I've built this house in hopes that I can have a wife and fill it with our children. It isn't good that man shall be alone—don't the Scriptures say that? I miss the six years of bliss that I had as a married man, and I'm lonely here by myself."

Ruth turned and walked away; Causes to Laugh looked after her daughter and then turned to Johnny, "She still loves no one but you! She's almost completely over her fears, you know." Cheryl entered the room, seeing Johnny with Causes to Laugh.

"I'm sorry. I hope that I didn't interrupt you all." She started to leave, but Johnny stopped her.

"I'm headed for my apartment, as I need to get a bath and to clean up. Tomorrow will be a busy day, as I've so much preparing to do for the wedding, and I need to go to the church to help Nina get the auditorium ready for the wedding. It's good to see you again, Causes to Laugh, and you too, Johnny." Then Cheryl was gone.

Johnny was about to go to his room when Ruth came back, and Causes to Laugh said, "I think you two need to talk."

She left, and Johnny said, "I hear so many good things about you, Ruth, honey, I'm so glad that you are doing well. You're beautiful, you know. I still love you very much too."

"What about Cheryl, Johnny? Did my madness drive her into your arms?" asked Ruth.

"You know, Ruth, Cheryl was the first girl I ever kissed. She was sixteen, and I was eighteen, and both of us were wet behind the ears. I had it pretty bad, but her dad and mother separated us and sent her East to school, and I was sent to the Mission and to school there. Separation did the trick, for I met you, Ruth, and fell madly in love with you, and I still am and believe that you still love me. Ruth, I've built this house for either you or Cheryl—which will it be? Do you still love me? We both wanted children at one time, and I'm very sorry you had the difficulty that you had, but Ruth, I made a vow and that was 'In sickness or in health,' and I tried to live up to my marriage vow, but you wouldn't permit me. You tried to send me into someone else's arms and succeeded, for I've kissed Cheryl. I'm sorry that it happened. That is all! We had no adulterous relationship!"

"Oh, Johnny, I am so very sorry for what I've done, but I was sick, and that terrible fear that I had is in the past." She rushed into Johnny's arms, and he kissed her fervently, and she responded fully. He thrust her tenderly from him and whispered, "Oh Ruth, I'm in love with two girls. What am I going to do? I didn't plan this, nor did I at one time want Cheryl's love, but she's so good and lovely, and I feel that she loves me and I love her. What can I do?"

Tears were streaming down Ruth's face. She'd sent him into Cheryl's arms, but now she knew the full truth. He hadn't been unfaithful to her even though she'd divorced him.

She kissed him and wept. "I'm sorry, Johnny; I was so sick! What can I do to correct such a horrible mistake? I love you more now than I've ever loved you for staying true to me and the vow that we took before God and to each other. Forgive me?" she pleaded.

"Oh Ruth, I do forgive you, for you couldn't help being ill. I shouldn't have signed those divorce papers, so I'm at fault too. You must forgive me. This will break Cheryl's heart if I turn to you, and it'll break your heart if I turn to Cheryl. My heart is already broken, and I'm miserable. I need to go help Cheryl at the church, do you want to come?" continued Johnny. Ruth thought a moment and answered in the affirmative.

•

Tom and Melody McDowell came riding into town in a surrey, followed by twenty cowboys. Johnny had reserved one of his hotels for all the cowboys. Matt and Bess came with four cowboys, and they all stayed at the same hotel. Orders were given that there would be no drinking. Slim asked Johnny if he could have time off to see some of his old friends, and Johnny visited the crew himself to welcome them and to tell them where to eat as he had made arrangements for their food with restaurant owners. William came by, and the crew gave him a hard time, kidding him unmercifully. William just grinned, and when he could find some way to return the kidding, he did so.

William McDowell married Nina Ragan, and they left for parts unknown on their honeymoon. Johnny served as host to several couples, including Tom and Melody McDowell, who looked with wonder on his new house and his conglomerate. Tom spoke to Melody before they retired for the night after visiting with Johnny.

"Melody, we sure misjudged that boy. I should've seen in him a diamond in the rough. Cheryl is still in love with him and would marry him in a second but for Ruth. How in the world can this have a happy ending? Our daughter loves him!"

"Yes, my husband, our little girl has a problem on her hands, and it's something that they must work out. We stepped into their lives when we shouldn't have, and I'm to blame as much as you," said Melody sadly. "Let us put it into the hands of the One who knows best. Let's pray about it."

Tom and Melody said their good-byes to Johnny and to Cheryl and left for their home with the cowboys following behind. It'd been a holiday for all, and the cowboys were envious of William.

JOHNNY REMARRIES

Johnny sat up late into the night considering Cheryl and Ruth. *Who will I ask to marry me? My mother used to say, when you are considering a wife, look at her mother or her dad, for the girl will undoubtedly have a similar physical appearance when she gets older.* Causes to Laugh came into his mind; the Indian woman still had a lot of charm, and her beauty was very extraordinary. Ruth had her physical appearance, but her auburn hair she got principally from her dad, who was slim and hardy. Melody was the most beautiful woman that he had ever seen. Cheryl was the very image of her mother with her light brown hair and big blue eyes.

"Lord," cried Johnny, "help me!"

He held his Bible in his hand and turned in the scriptures to I Corinthians 7:10, "Let not the wife depart from her husband: and let not the husband put away his wife." She'd put him away, but she'd been so very sick, and now she was well. He sat and thought and prayed and went to bed thinking of his auburn-haired beauty. He'd been very satisfied with their marriage and had loved her so much. He awoke right at dawn and rolled out of his bed.

His mind was made up as he put several things together in the way of food and clothing and rode out of Amarillo into the grasslands.

It was mid-afternoon by the time he saw the Mission, and he rode directly to the stables behind the Mission building. He was in the process of taking the saddle, saddle blanket, and bridle off his Appaloosa when he heard someone climbing the ladder to the hayloft. He heard the sound of falling hay as hay was pitched into the manger from the loft. He started to climb the ladder when he saw the auburn hair and two very beautiful brown eyes smiling down at him.

"Welcome home, Johnny! I'm so glad to see you! Don't ever let anything drive you away from me again!" she said through the tears. "I'm so sorry I caused you heartache." She came into his arms, and he kissed her tenderly. *Yes, this is right and as it should be,* he thought.

Ruth led him from the barn toward the Mission, where he met Causes to Laugh and John Beasley with arms outstretched.

"Welcome, Johnny!" They noticed that he had his arm around Ruth, and she wasn't pulling away.

Johnny pulled Ruth into the large Mission room, and Causes to Laugh and John Beasley remained in the kitchen area of the Mission.

Johnny held Ruth at arm's length. "Ruth, darling, I believe you are completely well again. Is that true?" She shook her head yes.

"You never, ever, even though we signed papers, were divorced from me. I know why you did what you did. You loved me more than what a man deserves and tried to set me free from my marriage vows so that I might marry another. I almost succumbed to Cheryl's charm, as she is very beautiful. I believe that I could've had her as my wife if I'd asked her. But my love, we made an oath before God and witnesses, and it's still true that you are my wife. I want to remarry you, to set right the papers of the State of Texas, which will show that I'm legally your husband. Ruth, will you marry me again? I love you more than ever! God has tried me and found me true to his scriptures, and I've been true to you."

"Yes, Johnny! I'll trust God that the children we beget will be born without mishap. God will bless our union. I love you more than I loved you before."

•

It was the eighteenth of May, 1863, and at Champion's Hill in front of Vicksburg, Union forces under Grant met the confederate forces under Pemberton and fought a decisive battle. The Union seized eighteen guns, and the Confederates lost three thousand men and were driven from the field in defeat. One of those who fell that day was Corporal Thomas Raymond Ragan. Weakened by lack of food and provisions, Ray had faithfully remained at his post and had been pierced through with rifle shot just before his squad retired from the field. One shot had severed his right arm, and a second had struck him dead center about two inches below his heart. The blow threw him on his back, and there he remained until men with stretchers found him later that night.

It seemed a miracle that he had not died, for his arm continued to hemorrhage, and a piece of his lung was protruding from his back. A surgeon worked over him and amputated his arm and stuffed his lung back into his body. The holes in his chest and back were cauterized, and Ray was moved into a larger tent, where he was expected to die. But he survived the infection, his fever soared, and his lips cracked and bled, and Ray hung on. He just wanted to see Susan and the kids one last time.

"This one has a lot of will to live! Let's see, it has been a month now since he was wounded. We need his bed for someone who might get well, a Confederate Soldier, and from Texas! Release him and send him on home to die. I feel sorry for him, but what else can we do? Put him on a train and send him to San Antonio and let his family care for him," said the physician as he studied his chest and arm.

Corporal Thomas Raymond Ragan was sent unattended by train back to San Antonio to die. Mrs. Susan Ragan was notified, and she came with a wagon and two mules to welcome her husband home from the war.

What she found was not the jovial, happy young man who had left her with three children on a rundown farm. This bundle of rags had one arm, an emaciated body, and stared at her from eyes sunken into a yellow forehead.

"Hello, Susan. It's me." He coughed deeply and harshly, and the spasm racked his body, and pink blood formed in bubbles on his lips.

"I'm sorry. I didn't want you to see me like this. I'm here to die. I do want to see the kids before that happens, honey." With the help of their oldest son, Johnny, she managed to get him home and to bed. Once there, wrapped in an old pair of his nightshirts, he immediately fell to sleep, completely exhausted from his trip.

Susan lay down by his side, and as he coughed and wheezed, she cringed and cried. In the middle of the night, she awakened in a cold sweat; a sharp pain was in her breast that ran down her left arm. Pains continued into her jaw, in her back, and she knew what it was, for this was not new but more severe than ever before. Lying there, she reached to touch him, but he coughed so harshly that she pulled back her hand.

"Johnny, oh Johnny! Come quickly! It's your mother! Johnny!" All three of the children came to stand at the edge of the bed.

"Son, get your horse, and ride to your uncle Clement's and bring him quickly."

Johnny was soon back, leading his uncle. The family stood weeping as their mother coughed and gagged and tried to live.

•

Susan Ragan was buried in a pine box behind the house. Her death was followed, three days later, with the death of Corporal Thomas Raymond Ragan. Following the burial of Susan, the corporal called his three children to his bedside, and between spasms of coughing, told his children that upon his death he wanted them to go to his brother's home to live there.

His brother, Clement, was a blacksmith and had a small farm just north of the Thomas farm. "Johnny, I want you to keep the Grulla, as she is your horse. Help take care of Nina," the corporal instructed.

Now, Clement Ragan was not too happy to become encumbered with three extra mouths to feed. His eyes wandered to the horse that Johnny claimed for his own. It would bring a hundred dollars with the bridle, saddle blanket, and saddle.

The second day after the burial of Thomas, Clement arose early and went to the stable and saddled the Grulla. He planned to take the horse into San Antonio to sell her. Johnny had gone back to his home to milk and had walked the quarter of a mile to the farm.

Johnny came into the yard carrying a bucket of milk and caught Clement about to mount his Grulla. "Where are you going with my horse?"

"Sorry, Johnny, but we need the money to feed you kids. I have to sell her!" answered Clement. Now Johnny was only eleven but big for his age, whereas Clement was rather puny and sickly.

"Uncle Clement, you know that dad and mother gave me this horse, and it is all I have to remember them by. Dad said for me to keep her, and that is what I intend to do." He reached forward with his right hand and seized the bridle.

"Let go of that bridle, Johnny. You are big enough to start earning your own way in life. You don't have a home with me! Get your clothes and get out! I'm going to sell this horse to help pay for Nina and Sam. Let go, hear?"

With all his might, Johnny hurled the two-and-a-half-gallon bucket of milk. The blow unseated Uncle Clement, and he fell backward into the manure of the manger. Johnny stepped over the senseless body of his uncle, mounted his horse, and rode to his home for his clothes and some food. After explaining the trouble to Nina and Sam, Johnny mounted his horse and rode toward San Antonio.

•

The loss of any possible revenue was a blow to Uncle Clement; he proceeded to take revenge on Nina and Sam. Nina inherited all the housework, which she willingly did, and became a good cook and housekeeper. Sam was young, but he milked the cow and tended to the three work horses left on the farm. His schooling began the day that Johnny left. Uncle Clement planned to get all he could out of Sam. He would teach him to be a blacksmith.

THE STRENGTH AND CHARACTER OF SAMUEL

Thanks to Nina, Samuel was fed well and grew tall; the constant work with a hammer enlarged his arms, and his chest expanded. Now Clement knew blacksmithing, and he taught harshly and sternly. Clement and Sam not only shoed horses but built wagons and buggies. Customers came out from San Antonio to see the merchandise built by this young giant. It was not Clement they came to see, but the strength of the young smith! He was the artist behind the "Ragan Wagons and Buggies." He loved horses, and his skill as a farrier became well known due to his tenderness with the animals.

No one could beat him in arm wrestling. He could bend a horse-shoe before it was heated. Many came to see this feat and marveled at his strength. They would often bring their champion, and Sam out arm wrestled them all. His strength became well known due to an accident which occurred near his forge. A runaway team had caused a coach to dump its passengers along the trail. The heavy coach pinned the coach driver beneath the upset vehicle. The driver's life was ebbing, but Sam put his massive shoulder under the coach and lifted the thousand pound coach until others could get to the man and pull him free.

A reward was sent to Sam from the coach company, which Sam refused to share with Uncle Clement. He paid Nina's tuition at a school in San Antonio, and she shared her knowledge with her brother, and so they cared for one another. That was the way it was in Texas, following the war, so many families were torn apart by the war. Two million men lost their lives fighting for the South and Texas had its share.

Nina insisted that Sam read the family Bible, and they shamed Clement into bowing his head while Nina or Sam had prayer for their meals. Clement developed consumption and became thinner as the days went by. Nina doctored him to the best of her ability, but it became clear that Uncle Clement would go the way of all flesh.

"This is the end of all men," said Nina. "Sam, we need to give him a decent burial. Let us bury him behind the house here. He wasn't a man who cared about anyone but himself, but I am thankful he gave us a place to live. He taught you a way to make us a living, and you are the best of any farrier that I know. Sam, let us stay here; I will cook and keep house, but you will need to provide food for the table."

•

One day, a well-loaded wagon pulled into the forge. On the side of the wagon was painted *Johnny Ragan's Freight/Hauling.* The teamster was rough and nearly toothless. He talked with Sam and asked that his wheels be packed for they were squeaking. Nina came out of the house and found that the freight company did business in Amarillo, Texas.

"Could this be our Johnny?" she asked Sam. The teamster had described his boss to Nina and Sam as being a large, hard man with curly black hair. He also owned a lot of property and was into the banking business. After the freighter had gone Sam thought a while, and said to Nina, "I have four hundred dollars, which I will split with you. You go to Amarillo and find Johnny. On the twenty-second day of April, 1889, the Indian lands of Oklahoma will be given to any American citizen. It will cost me nothing to ride into that new state and secure some land for us. The Indians named this land *Oklahoma* which means—in their language— *Beautiful land.* This opportunity to get first crack at the best lands only comes once in a lifetime. I will try to look you up in Amarillo as soon as possible after I can obtain a place. I will write to you at general delivery in Amarillo."

Nina agreed but wept over her younger brother; still, it seemed the right thing to do. Sam had a riding horse, a pack mule, and helped his sister catch a train in San Antonio for Amarillo. The second week of March he packed his mule, saddled his horse, and rode away from his home. It was his first trip away from home; he had taken many a wagon a day's journey from home to deliver the product of his making. But this was different; he would not return home again. Home now was on the back of his horse, the wide skies of Texas were the roof of his bedroom, and a small fire was the only warmth in lieu of the cheery hearth.

FORT WORTH

Several days into March, Sam came to the Trinity River, which was wild flowing and required a lot of skill to cross. He crossed where the trail had led him, but the horse could not swim across the raging waters, and Sam would have drowned were it not for some drovers who were crossing just ahead of him. They saw his plight and lassoed Sam as he was going down for the third time.

Dripping wet and completely water logged, Sam was pulled from the roaring waters.

"Thanks! I thought that my time had come. There is no such water near my home, and I've never learned to swim. I thought my horse would take me across," explained Sam to a ring of smiling cowboys.

"We thought you had bitten off more than you could chew too!" drawled one cowboy as he recoiled his rope.

Sam was trying to coral his mule, which had his forge on it and other tools of his trade. When he had the mule in check, he approached the cowboys to ask if he could camp with them for the night. "Sure can! We have a horse or two that is nearly lame and could use some of your attention."

Sam set up his forge and opened a bag of coal, which he soon turned into a hot fire. He had plenty that wanted to help, but Sam shooed them away, and soon he demonstrated his skill in horse-shoeing. After the fire had gone out, Sam shared some of his food with them and taught them how to arm wrestle.

Sam sat down by Wayne Wilson, the man who'd pulled Sam from the river, and Wayne began to question Sam regarding his trip into Oklahoma.

"Have you been to Fort Worth yet, Sam?"

"I'm not exactly sure where Fort Worth is."

"General William Worth gave the fort the name. He was a great man who made a name for himself during the Mexican war. General Harney named this place after General Worth. The fort is about a mile from here and is situated on a bluff overlooking the river. In the place is a hell hole of corruption known as 'Hell's Half Acre,'" stated Wayne.

"Now 'hell's half acre' is a rare name! Devil live there?"

"I'm not sure that he does, but I do know that a lot of his imps hang out there!" said Wayne with a chuckle. "We cowboys have had a lot of fun when we drive our cattle along this Chisholm Trail, and then we stop again on the way home. I bet you can make a bundle there, for there's sure to be some gambler who has his favorite and will want to bet against your arm wrestling. It is about time that we cowboys clean up on that bunch, for I've never seen anyone who can beat you. My arm will be sore for a week. Would you mind setting a time, so we can all make a trip into town and lift a buck or two off those gamblers?" Wayne grinned.

Other cowboys were gathering around and smiling at the thought of such a trip. They were digging into their pockets to see what they could raise for the bet and were smiling in anticipation.

"It is late to make a trip at this time of night, isn't it?" asked Sam.

"You kidding? Things haven't even begun going good in Duke's Saloon. Tell you what we will do! You arm wrestle and win, and we'll reward you with part of our winnings."

The crew ate their beans and steak, and, after the dishes were finished, they washed themselves and combed their hair. This seemed to be an extra-special event. They hung close to Sam and climbed the cliff to the fort. A challenge came from the guard on duty, and each identified himself. Wayne introduced Sam to the guard. Permission was granted for the crew to enter Fort Worth.

Duke's Saloon was situated in a prominent place at the center of a well-lit group of saloons. It was evident that they were in Hell's Half Acre. The piano was almost bouncing as music was cranked out of the machine. It was the first time Sam had seen a piano that ran off of rolls of paper that were indented and produced music from a cylinder. He stood for a minute, enchanted by the piano. There were several ladies who approached the cowboys. Each was sparsely clad and had painted faces. Some were pretty, but most were well worn, hard, and blemished.

Wayne came, surrounded by cowboys, followed by a dark man dressed in a three-piece suit.

"This is Duke, who has heard that you are good at arm wrestling and has a champion who is the saloon's bouncer, Andrew. But Sam, Andrew is at least three hundred pounds of muscle and as hard as a rock. He can lick any man I've seen. When Duke says throw him out, Andrew just picks up the *hombre* and bodily throws him out. Duke, how about odds? Can we have four to one?" Duke looked at Sam. Now, Sam had on a heavy coat, and his muscles were well hidden. The cowboys were standing around trying to hide the smiles on their faces. They were fingering their money.

"Three to one!" agreed Duke.

"Done!" said Wayne. Money came out of the cowboys' pockets by the handfuls. Sam pulled two hundred dollars from his pocket. Duke stepped back for the first time; he looked a little unsure, but he stuck with his agreement. One of the gamblers in a gray suit took down various amounts and gave receipts to each cowboy, including Sam's two hundred. The saloon showed interest now in Sam. A solid oak table was pulled into the center of the room with two of the bar room chairs. Sam took off his coat, and there was a whisper that went through the saloon as Sam flexed his muscles.

Sam was introduced to Andrew, and Andrew snarled at Sam. Rules were set up that the winner had to press the hand of his opponent down flat on the table. Each man had to keep his elbow on the table. Both men sat at the table, and the umpire wrapped his hands about the hands of the wrestlers.

"Ready, set, go!" said a very greedy Duke.

Sam was looking straight into the eyes of Andrew and saw the look of amazement come into the bouncer's eyes.

Andrew was instantly lifted out of his chair, and his hand was laid flat on the table. His face turned very red, and anger flooded his face. Duke was as shocked as his champion and looked with awe at Sam. The saloon crowd burst into cheers.

The cowboys were all screaming and jumping up and down at their good fortune, and they rushed to turn in the proof of their bet. Sam got in line and collected more money than he had ever had at one time. Six hundred dollars in gold coin and green backs weighed in his pocket.

Several of the dance girls surrounded him and offered him drinks, while the cowboys continued to beat him on the back. Duke approached him with a cruel smile on his face.

"Where did you learn to arm wrestle like that? I know Andrew has a lot of strength, and it is the first time that I have seen him get beat in anything. You want a job? All you will need to do is arm wrestle and maybe help Andrew every once in a while. I'll give you 25 percent of the total winnings. What do you say?" asked Duke.

"I'm not planning on staying here; I'm goin' into Oklahoma on the rush and maybe get me some land. I will bring my sister up from Texas, and she is depending on me for a home. I can't let her down," answered Sam.

"A lot of folk have already rushed the hour, and are in Oklahoma right now hiding from the military. We call them 'sooners' for they have already jumped the gun," grinned Duke. "I've got a couple up there working for me and maybe if you and I can get a deal going; just maybe, I'll cut you in on a place in Oklahoma. I'll sell it to you cheap!"

Sam did not like this slick crook, for he appeared to be rotten to the core. Out of the corner of his eye he saw Duke wave for a certain dancehall girl to approach them, and he knew he was about to be tempted even further.

"Sam, this is the sweetest little dance girl I have. This is Millie, and men all around here are crazy for her charms. Millie, meet Sam." Duke smiled. "Sam, Millie would be available with your new job."

A Spanish girl with dark eyes, dark black hair, and an excellent figure extended her hand to him. Her smile reflected a set of white teeth, and she was truly a cut above the other dance girls. Sam saw immediately why the cowboys preferred her. Sam took her hand in his and started to kiss her hand as he had seen others do many times. He faltered and simply squeezed her hand.

"I'm pleased to meet you!"

"And you too, sir!" She spoke in broken English and with a Spanish accent. She smiled, and a dimple appeared in her right cheek. Sam was thinking what a shame it was that she was the type of girl she was. The thought caused him to pull his hand free from hers.

Sam turned on the ball of his foot and went to the door. Sam walked into the cool of the night. The temptations of 'hell's half acre' had nearly won, but Sam felt spiritually good and pure as he walked back toward the fort. He felt the six hundred secure in his pocket and wondered if money, won like he had, would buy anything worthwhile.

He heard the whisper of clothing and a step along the path and suddenly he was in a fight for his life. A man of huge weight and size was swinging a black jack at him. His sombrero was knocked from his head, and his clothes were torn by the slashing of a knife. But Sam fought back. His fist was buried into the pit of the attacking man's stomach. The attacker screamed in pain as Sam stomped on the man's instep. A second cross jab caught the man on his chin, and the fight was over.

A soldier loomed out of the dark with his gun held at the ready. "Sergeant of the Guard, post number three!" screamed the guard. A second soldier appeared.

"What happened here?" asked the sergeant. He held a light high and looked at the unconscious bouncer. "I've seen this guy before! Why, that's Andrew from Duke's Saloon! I've never seen him out cold like that. He usually is beating some soldier to within an inch of his life. You hit him with something?"

His arm went under Sam's arm, and he saw the blood and torn coat.

"Sergeant, do you think we shouldn't take him in and let the doc look him over?" asked the guard.

"Take his other arm, and we'll get him to the doc." At the gate they slowed enough to send two troopers back for the unconscious bouncer.

"Look for a knife and that sap of his; this guy may want to press charges against Andrew."

A GUEST OF THE ARMY

"Well, young man, you were lucky. That sap just got you a glancing blow, or I'd be treating you for a fractured skull. That heavy leather coat kept that knife out of your lungs! I'd say Andrew had it in for you! Yes, sir, a mighty lucky young man!" said the doctor to Sam.

There was a rap at the door, and Major William (Billy) Englebright came in. He walked to the examination table and sat down on a nearby stool. He held in his hands two sheets of a report as filed by the sergeant. He lifted his eyes and looked toward the doctor.

"A very fortunate young man!" The doctor nodded toward Sam and then turned back toward the major. "Andrew has overstepped the law tonight and tried to kill this young man. He missed with his sap but managed to knife him, which was saved, I believe, by his heavy leather jacket. The wound was superficial!"

"Major, this is Samuel Ragan from down San Antonio way and is headed for Oklahoma to get himself some land in the rush," continued the doctor. "Sam, this is the commandant of our fort, Major Billy Englebright."

Both men nodded to each other. The major was military through and through. He was about six-feet tall and had sandy hair and large eyebrows. His face was well tanned, and his eyes were a pale blue. His attention was riveted on Sam.

"Sam, we've had a lot of trouble with men going to Duke's Saloon and being carried back to the fort with busted heads. We've had a few knifed also, which has basically been more life threatening. We have had Andrew thrown in jail only to have him sprung within a day or two. You've knocked Andrew into an unconscious state, and we have him and his weapons. We want you to press charges on Andrew. It will remove a thorn from our side, and we can put him away for some time. Most of our men are only about a third the size of Andrew, and your fight with him is all about the fort.

"The first of April our whole troop will be going to Oklahoma to participate in policing the opening of that territory, and if you would stay and press charges, we'll see you are there on time," said the major.

"Sounds good to me, for I really believe Andrew had it in mind to kill me. You see, I had whipped him in arm wrestling at the saloon and won a large amount of money from Mr. Duke. I believe Andrew followed me to steal my money. It could have been at the request of Mr. Duke, but I'm not sure of that. Mr. Duke tried to get me to work for him at the saloon, but I refused, and it angered him," stated Sam.

"You whipped Andrew in arm wrestling? Now that is amazing! I believe my entire troop would like to have seen that." The major chuckled. Sam was escorted down to the brig, where he saw a very disgruntled Andrew stretched out on a bed. He turned his back to Sam when he saw who the visitor was.

"Andrew, the army wants me to press charges against you, and I am considering it. Were you told by Mr. Duke to attack me and try to steal my money?" Andrew never moved, and Sam saw immediately that he was not going to answer. Sam left the brig and went back to the cowboy camp, where he collected his horse, mule, and materials he had left at the camp. He returned to the fort, where the guard recognized him, and was escorted to the main parade grounds, then to an empty room, which would be his, pending his case with the judge. The major was working fast in bringing this case to the judge's attention.

An orderly knocked on his door. "Sir, the major requests your presence at dinner. His residence is the large log cabin at the end of the street. It will be a semi-formal affair, and I would recommend that you bathe, shave, and wear your best, for Wanda, his daughter, will be there. She is the sweetheart of our brigade. Dinner will be served at 1900 hours," called the orderly.

Sam, shaved and bathed and dressed in his best clothing and knocked gently at the major's door.

"I'll get it, Dad," spoke a female voice from the cabin's interior.

The door was opened by the most beautiful girl that Sam had ever seen. She had large, green eyes that were set wide apart, a pug nose, a few freckles, and sandy-colored hair. Sam immediately knew why she was the darling to the whole brigade.

"Good evening, miss, I am Sam Ragan," said Sam politely.

"Oh sure, come in, come in, we've been expecting you. I'm the major's daughter, Wanda Joy Englebright," she stated.

Sam turned to see the major, the doctor, and a captain sitting in a small parlor off the dining area. The three stood and voiced their greetings to Sam. The major introduced Sam to Doctor (a captain) George McGregor and Captain Henry Forrester. The doctor Sam had met before; he was middle-aged and, besides being a doctor, was a professional soldier. The other captain, Henry Forrester, was a professional soldier and in his late thirties, with blond hair and a mustache. He was ruddy complexioned and had an air about him that made Sam dislike him almost immediately. He was looking at Sam as if Sam was far beneath him. Sam thought that he would like to arm wrestle this captain.

Captain Henry Forrester approached Joy and took her from Sam's arm. He led her to a chair, and Sam was left among the guests without a place to sit. The move made Sam blush, and both Joy and the major had noticed.

"Here, Sam, sit here, for dinner is ready," stated the major. He led Sam to the table, where he indicated a chair next to where he would sit. "Doctor, you sit here. Joy, take your usual place, and Henry, sit there." Sam had to smile, for Henry was seated at the foot of the table, and Joy was seated across from Sam. Sam thought of the game they played called musical chairs.

Captain Henry Forrester was annoyed. *Does the major like me or does he dislike the captain?* He looked across the table, and Joy was trying to stifle a smile too.

"Joy, will you say grace, please?" requested the major.

Joy knew how to pray and did such an excellent job that Sam sat amazed when she had finished. All said "Amen" except Sam, who said, "Thank you."

"Are you a believer in Christ?" asked Joy.

"Yes."

The major was dishing food onto plates, and they were passed around until all had food.

Joy had eye contact with Sam several times.

"Your dad fought for the South?" she inquired.

"Yes, I'm from Texas, just north of San Antonia."

"We're originally from Ohio, and we all fought for the North," quickly stated Captain Forrester. Captain Henry Forrester was over his shock and saw a way to get into the conversation.

"Joy, our forces delivered a devastating blow at Vicksburg. We divided the rebels into two parts. General Grant's force was tremendous in inflicting destruction on the rebels. It would be soon that the North would inflict such blows that the southern boys would have to capitulate." He looked at Sam and smiled.

"Captain, we are not here to fight the war over again. Sam was too young to be a participant in any of the fighting. Texas fought us honorably and with a lot of might. She has no reason to hang her head in shame," said the major.

The captain blushed a deep red at being reprimanded by the major. Joy smiled again. Sam smiled too and thought, *I don't think she likes this guy any more than I do.*

"Sam, tell us more about yourself. Where did you get all the strength that my soldiers are talking about? I was told you can bend a horseshoe before it is heated. We know you whipped the bouncer at Duke's Saloon in arm wrestling and beat him when he attacked you near the fort," said the major.

"I was forced to learn the trade of blacksmithing by my uncle. My sister was such a good cook that with all the exercise and hard work, I was molded into a muscular guy, I guess. I've never been whipped in arm wrestling and few can bend that horseshoe. Many have tried but few succeeded," said Sam.

"That is only brute strength! How much schooling have you had? I've been to college and wish to go to West Point some day," quipped the captain.

Sam looked across the table at Joy, who had a very angry look on her face. "You'll never make it to West Point, for you might even flunk the physical," she said to the captain.

Sam covered his smile with his napkin. This girl was fiery! No wonder she was the delight of the brigade! The captain had been put into his place, and everything got quiet as the guests enjoyed their dinner.

Following the meal, Joy walked around the table and spoke to Sam. "I'm sorry we have such mealy-mouthed captains in this army. Dad should have fought for the confederate cause. I hear there was a lot of chivalry among their officers. Captain Henry Forrester is crude, insensitive, ignorant, and egotistical. I have to put up with this bore, and I'm sorry he said what he did," said Joy between clenched teeth.

She took Sam's arm and led him away from the frowning captain and into the parlor, where she selected two chairs away from the others and bid Sam to sit down by her.

"Thank you, Joy!" He really admired the grit in this girl and enjoyed very much being in her presence.

"Dad tells me you plan to go into Oklahoma on opening day. What will you be looking for? Commercial or residential land? Maybe you will be considering ranching? Do you plan to continue blacksmithing? Dad is always looking for a scout or extra men for this army post. I hear Dad talk about the Indian menace and the problems that are ahead. He will approach you in regards to joining the army. You mark my words! Don't listen to him; I'd never want to be married to an army man." Joy realized what she had said and blushed a deep scarlet. "Would you care for a coffee or perhaps a glass of wine?" she continued.

"No, thanks, I'm fine," said Sam. "I have no interest in joining the army." He smiled at her discomfort and wondered how he could remedy her remark to help her regain her composure. But Joy was looking at the captain, who was very interested in carrying over a chair.

"Quick, Sam, let us take a stroll outside and get away from that stupid captain. He is planning to interrupt our conversation. Oh, here he comes!"

Sam was on his feet and assisted Joy to her wrap. The captain looked on in dismay while Sam held her coat for her and escorted her out on the parade ground.

"Well done!" She laughed deeply. "Did you see the look of amazement that came to his face?"

"It is cold out here! We have a very cool April. Do you have enough clothing?" asked Sam. He reached for his leather jacket, which he put around her shoulders.

"Thanks," she replied.

"Now to the question about what type of land that I will be looking for in Oklahoma; I have really kicked this around in my mind. I can make a very good living as a blacksmith, but it doesn't have much of a future. I am waiting to hear from my sister, Nina, who is in Amarillo looking for my older brother, Johnny. We think he is in business there and has a good foot in the door. I have been looking for a letter from my sister and need to check to see if it was forwarded here."

"Your dad said he was going to Purcell and that I could go with the troop. I've heard that there is a special train scheduled to arrive there before the trumpet sounds, and people start crossing the river. It may be the way to do it, but I plan to have my horse and mule unrestricted and hope to get a good place among the million acres that are available," continued Sam.

"It sounds so very exciting, and my prayers go with you that you'll succeed. Sam, I am envious of you and the adventure that you have before you. I'm so cold; we must go in," she pouted.

"There they are!" said the major. "Sam, I want to talk with you, as I've a proposition to make. Come on in and sit down." Sam was led back to the parlor, where Joy brought him a steaming cup of black coffee. She sat near to Sam so she could hear the conversation.

"Sam, we need guys like you in my troop. I wish I could offer you a commission, but I cannot. There are good men in my troop that've been with me for ten to twenty years, and it'd be unfair to

JOE WAYNE BRUMETT

152

them for you to be offered a commission over them. I think you would make a good officer. How about coming to work for me in that capacity? I have several Indians who can track anyone across the desert. It is common sense that I need in my troop, and there're Indian wars that right now are about to commence," pleaded the major. "What do you say?"

Sam glanced at Joy, who had an "I told you so" look on her face.

"Sir, the adventure is appealing, but I have a sister who is awaiting my trip into Oklahoma. It would be unfair to her," stated Sam.

"A sister, you say? She is awaiting your adventure, seeking lands for her benefit as well as yours? I understand! If things do not turn out as you hoped then remember that the army could use you." The major smiled.

"Thank you, sir! And Joy, thank you for the dinner and the coffee. It has been a very pleasant evening," said Sam, smiling

She slipped out of his leather jacket, and he held her hand for a moment and kissed it. The event pleased her, and she smiled at him.

"Thanks!" he murmured so only she heard. He turned and went out into the night and back to his cabin.

●

The United States District court was in session. Whereas the crime was committed in a United States fort, William Slovic, bouncer at Duke's Saloon, was tried by a United States District judge and found guilty of attempted robbery, attempted murder, and use of a lethal weapon to commit a crime. Duke, not wanting to be connected with the crime, did not send his lawyers but let William take the blame and punishment for what he had done. The judge found him guilty and sentenced William to five years of hard labor in a United States Penal Institute. Sam had appeared as a witness against William, along with the doctor, the major, and the sergeant of the guard that came upon the scene. William was sent to Yuma prison to serve his time.

PURCELL, INDIAN TERRITORY

Major William "Billy" Englebright led his troop from Fort Worth to the city of Purcell, Oklahoma, just north of the area where a small city of tents, Conestoga wagons, and masses of awaiting people lingered in anticipation of finding a new home among the million acres to be given away by the government to the lucky folk that would stake it out and file a claim. The troop crossed the Canadian River and set up their tents in the restricted area. Sam was not permitted to cross and had to remain south of the river. There was a ford just north of Purcell, and Sam looked with a little fear at crossing there. He well remembered when he tried to cross the Trinity River and had to be pulled from the raging waters.

Sam set up a tent and got out his forge. He immediately had more work than he could handle. Everyone seemed anxious that their horse would make the trip without going lame. He shoed an average of fifteen horses a day and worked late into the night. He still had the six hundred that he had won arm wrestling but kept it hidden from view. He wondered often about Joy and made for the post office in hopes he had a letter from Nina.

On the twentieth of April, he received such a letter that indicated she had found Johnny and was working for him. Johnny had been married and was having marital difficulty with his Indian wife. Johnny was very rich and doing well in Amarillo, Texas. If Sam wished, he could come to Amarillo, and Johnny had work he could do there. *Write to us both,* she requested. She had met a fine young man and was planning to get married.

Sam held the letter in his hands and wondered about the trip looking for a place in Oklahoma. Nina would not need someone to care for her, for his sister was getting married! She had told how terrific her fiancée was and of the happiness she had found. They were building a house in Amarillo, as was Johnny.

Sam sat for a long time wondering what to do. *I've got no one but myself to look after now.* Suddenly he was filled with remorse and self-pity. His mind dwelt on Joy, and he thought of her rather often.

●

As time grew nearer, some tried to cross the river north of the ford. A wagon, several people, and all their supplies were swallowed up by the quick sands. No one knew how many perished or who they were, but the *New York Times* wrote an article of finding a young man who had drowned in the quick sands. Major William Englebright sent troops to try to prevent such events from happening and to keep the people to the south of the river. Many were trying to get an advantage and to get ahead of the crowd. No one knows how many perished in the waters and quick sands. As the day approached, Sam kept visiting the post office each day, hoping Nina and Johnny would write. Had they received mail he had sent?

●

On the twenty-second of April, he arose early and packed his blacksmith equipment on his mule. The troop was at the ford and on the northeast side. The trumpeter waited and stood at attention for a good fifteen minutes. The major gave the signal, and the horn was blown. Sam followed the crowd, and the fifty thousand plus rushed into the water. Sam was pressed on all sides until he was across the river. Many were ahead, but he set a steady pace, and before long the crowd thinned out.

He kept the Canadian River to his west, and after traveling several miles toward the end of the day, he turned north. He saw people every so often but knew he was ahead of most. He saw a few riders, but the wagons had been left far behind. He came across a few land markings and was sure they had been marked by 'sooners.' Dark was coming on, and he decided to mark an area while he could see. He picked out a well-drained area that had frontage on a lake, tied his horse, and paced off his boundaries. Each stake he worked on till there was no doubt to whom the land belonged. Samuel Ragan was clearly etched on each stake. It was dark when he was finished, made camp, fixed a meal, and fed his mule and horse. He fell asleep with rifle nearby. He was awakened by the sound of rolling wheels, and a Conestoga wagon lumbered out of the early morning fog.

"This is the place, and it fronts on the lake," came a voice from the wagon.

"Jason, someone has already staked this place." This was followed by a bit of profanity.

"I told you I should have ridden ahead and staked it off. We could have brought the wagon up later. Do you see who might have staked it?" called a voice that must have belonged to Jason.

"There is a camp over by that big tree and a man standing right there," answered another voice. "Maybe we can buy this place from him," called Jason.

Jason had his stakes in hand, and Sam watched him as he grabbed one of Sam's stakes as if to pull it up. Sam lifted his rifle and in a quiet voice said, "I don't think I would do that if I were you. I am within the law, and I rode hard yesterday to get here. There are many acres to the east and west that have not been staked. I don't want any trouble, but if you pull my stake you will find more trouble than you bargained for."

"I've got a bead on him, Uncle Jason! Do you want me to shoot him?" called a voice off to Sam's right.

"There will be no shooting here!" called a voice of authority. A deputy United States Marshall rode into view. Sam relaxed, and Jason voiced his opinion with more profanity and let go of Sam's stake.

"Who is Sam Ragan?" inquired the deputy.

"I am he!" stated Sam.

"You have staked this land according to law, and it is yours! Mister, don't pull up his stake, or he has a right to do you bodily harm. From the size of that guy you would not have a chance. I'm here to see that justice is done," said the deputy. Jason called to his mules, and they drove around the lake.

"Thanks!" called Sam.

"I believe I will stake the land to your right, and one of us can watch the other's land while we ride to have the land recorded. My name is Deputy Jon McRaffity."

"Thanks for the help, for we were about to get into a shooting match. Most of the lake is on me, but you can stake the balance of the lake, and we can have the lake within both our rights," called Sam. Jon had his stakes and was measuring off his land.

"This land lies as pretty as can be. I think we have selected some very prime land," called Jon. Both Sam and Jon had lunch together and stood watch while several more rode their wagons along the trail and looked at the staked property. The next day, Jon and then Sam rode back to have their lands recorded. Sam felt he had found a good, honest friend and really liked the Irishman. The trail, which fronted on Sam's property, was a thoroughfare, and Sam set up his forge and shoed several horses. Several were staking to the north, and a city was in the progress of being formed. Sam had been very fortunate in acquiring his land as to location, and he thanked the good Lord for His impute. Sam worked his mule and improved the road on the west side of his property. He hired men to construct a nice cabin overlooking the lake and used the last of his money from his arm wrestling to pay for the construction, so it was now free and clear.

He watched over Jon's lands while the deputy was away at work and offered Jon a loan so that Jon could build a cabin. The friendship grew, and the two men worked together in business and as good neighbors.

One day, as Sam was working at his forge, a man came in a buggy that had a squeaking wheel. As Sam greased the wheel, the customer was looking over Sam's place. When he came to Sam to pay for the finished job, he said to Sam, "I've been looking over your place and believe you have a prime place for a subdivision for Oklahoma City. I develop lands and would like to buy or lease some or all of your lands. Interested?"

"Maybe," said Sam. "I need to see Jon."

"I've checked up on Jon and have found that he could not file on this land due to his being a deputy and U.S. Marshall. He has found this out and has filed using your name. So, you own that place too," grinned the developer. "I heard that Jon plans to get out of police work and then he will ask you to sign the place over to him. That is smart of him, no?"

"I know nothing of such dealings! Jon would have asked me first," Sam said. This could be true, as he had not seen his neighbor for a couple of weeks. The thought bothered him so that he just stopped working on the buggy and sat stunned in his chair.

"It takes all kinds, doesn't it?" asked the developer. "If I were you, I'd ask Jon to sell it to you for a dollar and then really put it into your name." He grinned, and his yellow teeth showed through his lips. "I believe you can get a clear deed."

Sam dropped his head as he finished packing the buggy's wheels.

"Give me a few days to check out what you have told me, and let me talk with Jon. I need to study up on what I should get to lease this place. I'm not sure what is fair. Drop by again next Wednesday and bring your papers. I'll need to see a lawyer," said Sam.

The developer shook Sam's hand and drove away, well satisfied with the work Sam had done on his buggy. Sam had checked often when he went into Oklahoma City if he had mail from Nina or Johnny. He had two letters from Nina and one from Johnny. Nina was now Mrs. William McDowell, and they were living in Amarillo. William was working for Johnny as an engineer. Johnny had built a nice home in Amarillo and owned an assortment of businesses. Johnny and his Indian girl were expecting their first child. From Nina's letter, Johnny and his wife had three miscarriages, and it had caused grief among them.

"Pray for your brother and his wife, Ruth, that they might have a healthy child," wrote Nina. "I, too, am looking for a little one, and we are thrilled to death. William and I are very happy. I sing in the choir with Johnny, and Ruth plays our organ at church. Sam, you would do well to live here. Do you have any special one? Be happy, my brother, be happy."

Johnny's letter seemed like a letter from a stranger. Sam wondered what Johnny looked like. Johnny was telling him about the various people who worked for him and their roles in his conglomerate.

"I have plenty of places where you can work, but little brother of mine, you are a stranger to me, and I do not know your interest. We need to get acquainted again. You just come and visit with us anytime, if you wish, and let's see what your interests are."

Sam resealed both letters and sat at his forge, wondering just what his true interest was. His mind went back to Jon and then to the report he had received from the developer. Jon was a great guy, and he wouldn't cheat nor take advantage of him. That was Sam's conclusion.

On Monday, about noon, Jon came riding down the lane.

"We have some talking to do, Jon," said Sam. Sam told him what had been told by the developer. Jon looked sick and said it was true. At his work, the United States Marshall had gotten word that Jon had filed and told Jon that he could not file according to law. There had been others that had tried it and failed. Jon asked the marshall if he could sell the property to Sam since the property had been filed on by Jon, and they had not caught the error,

"You want to buy my spread for a dollar and then sell it back to me for a dollar?" asked Jon.

"I have heard of all kinds of deals. Most officials are looking the other way until the land trades hands a time or two. Then, who cares, at least they seem to be saying that," said Sam. "Jon, what would you think if I leased my land to this developer? I could have a steady income for years to come. I am planning to make a trip to Amarillo to visit with my brother and sister. I want to lease this property before I go so it won't cause me concern while I am there. Johnny, my brother, owns some banks in Amarillo, and I will let them be responsible to see that the leases are paid."

"Sam, I'll miss you, and my prayers will go with you," said Jon.

Sam got a better deal with the leases than he thought he would and said payments would be sent to Ragan National Bank and in Samuel Ragan's name. The leases were made for fifty years, and Sam's lawyer had them recorded. The lawyer recorded Jon's sale to Sam and then Sam's sale back to Jon.

Jon watched Sam as he turned his horse and mule south and, within a couple of days Sam was back at Fort Worth. He rode to the fort gate and was challenged by the guard who remembered Sam for his arm wrestling. The major was not at the fort, but he and his troops were in Colorado in battle with the plain Indians. Joy had left the fort and was in San Antonio visiting with family friends. No one had her address, so Sam turned his horse and mule toward Amarillo.

It had been rather safe riding up till now, but he was now riding into Indian territory. He bought a new Winchester 44, and several boxes of shells. He also bought a Colt 44 so shells could be used in either gun. He found a trail heading west and watched the trail and guarded his back trail. For three days he saw no one but was very careful with his campfires and tried to keep hidden from view.

An Indian party was sighted on the fourth day, and he hid from them in a deep ravine. The party was a hunting party, for he saw no war paint. He was not an expert in Indian lore but thought they were Cherokee, and that was not an educated guess. There were about twenty in the group, and there were no children or women. He built no fire that night and climbed a tree after dark to check his back trail. The fire of the hunting party was seen clearly about a mile on down the trail east of him. He ate some dried jerky for breakfast, and the fourth day of his journey was uneventful. Wanting some warm food, he found some dry wood and built a very small fire. He opened a can of beans, peeled some potatoes, and camped just off the trail near a small, clear steam. He was lifting his first spoonful of beans to his mouth when his mule whinnied, and was answered by a whistle from the trail, followed a minute or two later by a second whistle. Both of his animals were looking toward the trail, so he reached for his Winchester.

Sam waited, holding his breath; he slipped off his heavy riding boots and put on a pair of moccasins. His eyes did not leave the

JOE WAYNE BRUMETT

160

trail. His horse and mule were hobbled, so he moved to his left and soon came to the trail. He saw movement ahead, and there was a lone Indian, mounted, and holding the nostrils of a second horse.

Sam held his rifle on the Indian until the Indian saw Sam. Would he reach for a weapon? Both Sam and the Indian looked at each other. The Indian had the same questions regarding his security. The Indian raised his hand as a sign of peace and friendship. Sam was suspicious but lowered his gun.

"Do you speak English?" asked Sam. The Indian did not move, so Sam walked toward his camp and motioned for his guest to follow. When Sam arrived at the fire, he indicated for the Indian to get off his horse and sit with him at the fire. The Indian complied.

"I am Big Beaver, and I scout for the army," he said. "I'm of the Nez Perce Wallowa Tribe and my chief is Joseph. I have been to San Antonia with two of my horses, one I have bred. They are Appaloosa, you see," said the Indian.

"They are very fine horses; are they for sale or trade?" Sam asked. "I have heard of your chief and of his seeking peace with the white man. He is well known among our people."

"You and I must be very alert, for I have been followed by a hunting party the last five miles. I am unsure just who they are, but our tribe has many enemies. Our horses are in demand, and so the party that follows me may have in mind to steal my horses," said the Indian.

Sam saw the four horses lift their heads and look toward the trail. He motioned to Big Beaver, and the Indian pulled a rifle from a gun boot and moved to a large tree. Sam was impressed with the quiet manner in which the Indian stalked danger. There was movement at the trail, and several Indians on foot moved toward the camp.

"They are Pawnee," spoke Big Beaver. He lifted his rifle and shot an approaching warrior. Sam covered him while he reloaded his gun. Sam's new rifle was a sixteen-shot repeater, and Sam managed to hit a half dozen stalkers before they turned and fled.

"Good shooting! We may have punished them more than their desire to have the horses," said Big Beaver.

"How did you know they were Pawnee?" asked Sam.

"See their top knots! That one right there has the head of a wolf. They use the skin of a wolf and try to slip up on a campfire to kill campers as they sleep. Our tribe, as well as many others, do not like their ways and do not worship their gods. They try to steal our children and our wives. We often battle with them. These were after my horses and our scalps." He pulled a knife from his belt, and Sam turned his back as Big Beaver scalped the six Indians that had been slain.

"Do you think they will try to attack us tonight?" asked Sam.

"If they are a part of a larger group, they may seek help from them and return tonight. Your gun may well have discouraged them, and then again they might want it for their own," said Big Beaver.

"You think we should move our camp?" asked Sam.

"I believe that we have a good area to defend ourselves. You have chosen a good campsite, and I believe I owe you my life, for it was the rapid fire of your Winchester that stopped them," smiled Big Beaver.

Sam finished cutting his potatoes, and they ate together. It was evident that Big Beaver had eaten white man's food before. They shared guard duty, and from the smiles on his face, Sam believed he had found a true friend.

Four days they traveled together, and Sam's confidence in Big Beaver grew. On the fifth day, about noon, Big Bear pulled up the horse he was riding. The trail forked here, and Big Beaver looked to the trail, which headed South.

"My friend, this is where we must part; I must travel to the North, and your path heads south. You should reach your destination in about two day's time. If you err and miss the town of Amarillo, you will run into railroad tracks that will lead you back to the town. The Indians in this area are mostly peaceful, so don't be afraid to trade with them. My path is long, and I fear that my people will have war with the white man. Chief Joseph is a peaceful man, and the spirit of peace is in him. I find it sad to say goodbye to you. I want you to remember me; please take my friend here with you." He held out a rope bridle of the Appaloosa he'd been riding.

"He is broken to bridle and saddle; you will never remember the Indian name I gave him when he was born, so you may want to give him a white man's name. Good-bye, Samuel."

Sam took what he believed to be the most precious possession Big Beaver owned. The Indian had turned north, but Sam stopped him. "This gun saved our lives once, and I give it to you to protect you and keep you safe. These shells are 44 caliber, and I give you over half that I own." Sam held out his new Winchester and gun belt for Big Beaver to take. Big Beaver smiled his thanks. "Good trade." He smiled, and then he turned and rode his mare up the trail.

"May the great spirit go with you, Samuel, my friend." Sam sat on his horse holding the rope bridle until Big Beaver was out of sight. He took saddle, blanket, and bridle from his horse, and while talking to the Appaloosa managed to get the horse saddled and bridled.

The horse trembled for a few minutes when Sam mounted, and Sam had the bridles of his mule and horse as he started south. Sam was especially careful relative to his campsite, for he had no rifle, and he was not a great shot with his pistol. On the third day after leaving Big Beaver, Sam rode into Amarillo.

•

Ragan National Bank was an extra large building, and Sam tied his horses at a rail in front of the bank. He walked into the bank and was met by a guard.

"Good morning, Mr. Ragan," spoke the guard. Then he stopped and looked again. "Oh, I'm sorry, but I see that you are not Mr. Johnny Ragan."

"I'm his brother, Samuel! Does he have an office in this building?"

"No, but our bank manager will want to see you. Her office is on the second floor; just take those stairs, and her office is on the right," said the guard.

Samuel stood stunned as he admired the beauty of the building and the solid marble floors. Several customers were at the cashier cages. Sam stood at a door that had a name on it. "Cheryl McDowell, Manager." He rapped lightly on the door, which was opened by a dark-haired girl.

"Mrs. McDowell?" questioned Sam. The girl was startled, and her mouth opened as she looked at Sam.

"You are the spitting image of Johnny Ragan," the girl said.

"I'm his brother, Samuel."

The door to her private office opened, and a very pretty brown-haired lady, with large blue eyes, came into the outer office. She stood for several seconds and appraised Samuel.

"How very rude of me; I'm Cheryl McDowell and it is as Betty says, you look exactly like Johnny Ragan. Please come into my office! We have received some leases that have been sent here, so we knew you were coming." She smiled, and Sam was enchanted by the beauty of her smile and straight, even teeth.

"Please, Lord, let her be single," Sam prayed silently.

Cheryl had recovered her poise and composure. "Samuel, will you be staying in our community? Are you married, and do you have a family?" Her blue eyes were fixed on him.

"I have no wife, could never find anyone who wanted me."

That wasn't the right way to answer her! He thought and bit his tongue. She smiled and went to the window.

"That large building in the middle of the block is Mr. Johnny Ragan's office building. He will be there for another hour, and the office building will close for the day. Have you seen him since you arrived?" she asked.

"I haven't seen my brother in fourteen years and don't have the vaguest idea what he looks like."

"If you look in a mirror you will see what Johnny looks like. We will be balancing books, or I would take you to his office," said Cheryl.

"Thank you, Mrs. McDowell."

"Miss McDowell," she corrected and smiled. There, he had his answer, and he was captivated by this lady.

Sam easily found Johnny's office building and realized that Johnny used the entire second floor for his offices. He was led to his inner office, and there stood his brother; in the outer office was his sister, Nina.

Sam was embraced by Nina and then by Johnny.

"We are all together again, and I hope we will never be apart," said Johnny. "You sure have gotten to be an ugly kid!"

"I've heard it said that we look alike!" Sam grinned.

"Nina, you look very beautiful. Who is this William you married?"

"You said you met Cheryl. Well, William is her twin."

"I bet that he is not as pretty as his sister! She is the most beautiful woman I have ever seen." Sam smiled. He was thinking of Joy when he made the statement. Joy was second best now.

"You haven't seen Ruth, Johnny's wife, yet," said Nina. "This place is full of very pretty girls."

"I'm looking forward to meeting as many as I can."

Johnny called a man from the outer office and introduced him to Johnny.

"Johnny, this is my bodyguard, Slim Wilkins. Don't ever pick a fight with him, for he will shoot the buttons off your shirt. He saved the life of William and Cheryl's dad in a gunfight. He is a special friend to us all and helps keep peace in my company," drawled Johnny. Johnny wrote a note to Pierre and asked Slim to carry the note to the cook so he would know how many to prepare dinner for that evening.

Slim and Sam shook hands, and Sam liked Slim almost immediately. Slim took the note and left.

"What are you riding?" asked Johnny.

"Had an Indian give me an Appaloosa, which I have not named yet. I also have my horse left over from when Uncle died. She isn't the greatest but has been very loyal to me. Have a mule too. I rode them down from the bank, and they are tied out front of your office."

"I, too, have an Appaloosa, and by the way, he too was given to me by an Indian," said Johnny. "I have a good manger, so follow me." Johnny led the way, and Sam was amazed to see Johnny's name on so many buildings. His home was the largest home in town and looked brand new. Johnny took Sam to the manger, where an older caretaker took the horses, telling Johnny he would wash them down after they were cooled off.

Johnny introduced Sam to Ruth and their daughter, Naomi. What Nina had said about Ruth was true. She was an exceedingly beautiful woman. She had auburn hair, brown eyes, and was petite. Her eyes danced with happiness as she offered her hand to Sam.

"I had no idea that you would look so much like Johnny. Sam, Naomi is very special to Johnny and I, for she is the first child that I have been able to carry to term. The Lord, our God, has blessed us so very, very much." A tear came into her eye, and Sam knew there was more but did not pry.

Johnny was taken to the guest room, and after a hot bath and shave he dressed in one of Johnny's suits.

●

The bell built into the front door rang, and Ruth answered the door. Several voices were heard speaking greetings. Sam put the finishing touch on his black tie and slipped on his coat. He had been changed from the man of the trail to a well-dressed gentleman. He did look very much like his brother.

Cheryl was standing in the hall and staring at him. She blushed slightly when she realized she was staring and that he was watching her.

"I'm sorry, but you look so much like Johnny that it amazes me." She recovered her composure.

"You know, before Johnny married Ruth, I had a crush on him. He gave me my first kiss." She grinned.

William was led forward by Nina, and she introduced her husband to Sam. He could see very little resemblance between William and Cheryl. Amos DeJohn and Red Doe made a fine appearance. Slim Wilkins introduced Mildred Wilson, his fiancé from town. Rex and Erma Hammond were there, and Sam immediately liked the couple.

"Dinner is served in the dining area," stated the maid. Ruth told each where to sit, and sure enough Sam was seated across from Cheryl. Sam looked across at Johnny and winked. Johnny was trying to encourage something; Ruth was smiling too. Johnny prayed a very excellent prayer, and thanked God not only for the food, but good friends, and the happiness of having his family with him.

The evening was an excellent one, and finally each of Johnny's good friends excused themselves and left.

"Sam, my buggy is outside. Would you mind seeing Cheryl back to her apartment?" asked Johnny.

"I'd be happy to," said Sam. Sam was an expert with horses and very shy with women. He was a little surprised when Cheryl moved closer to him in the buggy.

The apartment was only three blocks away, and Sam didn't want to end the evening with a short, two-block ride.

"Would you like to see some of the town? There wouldn't be anyone out on the street, and I can show you some of Johnny's holdings," suggested Cheryl.

"I'd like that!"

"Johnny holds a commanding interest in that railroad. That is his Ragan Freight and Hauling. He owns that Mercantile Store. Yonder is his lumber and brick works. He owns three banks and the apartment where I live. Of course, there is his office building and his construction companies, which my brother runs for him. I try to keep his banks in line, and he is a man of abundant wealth."

Sam sat speechless as he thought of all the property his brother owned. He had in his pocket a hundred dollars that he thought made him rich. He would reveal his poverty when he deposited the money in the bank tomorrow. Why not display it now?

"Cheryl, I am near poverty! I own some horses and have property near Oklahoma City, which is leased for fifty years. I have one hundred dollars, which I will deposit in your bank tomorrow. But I sleep well and have good health and haven't a worry in the world. That is something to be thankful for."

They were in front of her apartment, and he pulled the buggy to a stop and dropped a weight that would keep the horse from wandering.

"Sam, thanks for seeing me home." She reached over and gave him a peck on his cheek and turned and ran up the steps to her apartment. Sam sat there for a minute or two and got out to lift the weight from the bridle of the horse. He rode to the manger, where he took the bridle and carriage gear off the horse and parked the buggy.

•

Sam had always been an early riser and was up at the crack of dawn. Johnny was at breakfast, and Ruth was feeding the baby.

"Johnny placed a cup of steaming brew before him.

"What have you got for me to do this morning?" asked Sam.

"What do you want to do?"

"Johnny, have you ever heard of Chief Joseph, who is chief of the Nez Perce tribe?"

"A year ago, he whipped the army in a couple battles up in Montana. He was the best chief that the Indians had and was thought to be a chief wanting peace with the army, but the army didn't want peace with him. I think they chased him until they caught up with him, and the chief whipped the army good. His dad was a good Indian and was named Joseph by a missionary. The younger Joseph had a name, which in our language meant Thunder Rolling in the Mountains. They originally came from the Wallowa Valley and raised Appaloosa horses. These were beautiful animals, and when I fought the Indians that were attacking the mission where Ruth's dad was missionary, Indians nearly beat me to death and killed my Grulla. When I finally came to, Chief Red Hand gave me an Appaloosa to replace my Grulla. I still have that Appaloosa and believe that the horse originated from the Nez Perce Tribe," said Johnny.

"On my way from Oklahoma I met an Indian named Big Beaver, and he and I had a battle with a hunting party; I used the rapid fire of a Winchester to repulse them. When Big Beaver and I were about to part, he gave me his Appaloosa, and not to be outdone, I gave him my Winchester. That horse really means a lot to me, and it was not difficult to make a real pet out of him. You know that I am a farrier, as our uncle taught me all he knew. I have also been making coaches and wagons and had a good business there in San Antonio," stated Sam.

"Now that's hard work!" stated Johnny. "I would like to make you into a real gentleman who oversees other workers. I could get in touch with my father-in-law and have you teach a class in blacksmith. They have many Indians who are excellent workers with their hands. You could get several good workers and make a good business for them and for you."

"That's a good idea, Johnny! Would I need to go to the mission to do this?" asked Sam.

"They would be tickled to death to have the class taught there, and just maybe some of his teaching might rub off on you," said Johnny.

Sam smiled. "It would not hurt to learn a little more about the Bible. I could put some of their designs on my wagons and buggies, too."

"Need any cash to help you start your business?" asked Johnny.

"Financially, I'm better fixed than I have been in some time. Have you got an area where I could put my forge and set up a show room for my product?" asked Sam.

"Sure, I might manage that."

"That Cheryl is such a beautiful girl, Johnny, but I wonder if she is in love with someone who looks like me. She sure didn't give me much encouragement last night," declared Sam.

"Give her time, Sam! She is worth waiting for," Johnny said softly.

•

Sam saddled his Appaloosa and rode to the bank, where he deposited his one hundred dollars. He asked to see Cheryl and was led to her outer office. She offered him a peck on her cheek and took him into her office, where he sat in front of her desk. She seemed slightly distant and cool to him. This really puzzled him.

"Cheryl, I would like for the bank to assist me with a group of leases that I have near Oklahoma City. These are land leases, and they are for fifty years."

"We have had this paperwork for about a month now, and it was a clue to us here at the bank that you would be coming into this area. We will be most happy to service your leases for you and collect your rent. You've excellent leases, and they should provide a nice income."

Sam got up to leave, and Cheryl came forward and took his big hand in hers. "Sam, welcome to Amarillo! Everyone that I have seen have expressed how much you and Johnny look, speak, and act alike. We all love Johnny so much, and it is good to have two of him around here," said Cheryl. "Oh, thanks again for seeing me home and being such a gentleman."

"Cheryl, I want to see you again, but I need to make a business trip to the mission field, for I plan to start a class among the Kiowa in blacksmithing. I plan to begin such a field of work in Amarillo and make wagons and buggies."

"Excellent thought. You will be going to the mission field soon?"

"I want to do an errand for Johnny and see a lot of this country. Johnny wants me to take a deed down to Matt and Bess for the property that he sold them. Johnny wants me to visit with your folks and get acquainted with the TM Ranch. I'm heading south for a few days and then will head back north and on to the mission field. I'm leaving right after lunch, today; I want to take you to dinner when I return."

"Let me write a line or two to my dad and mom!" said Cheryl. She went to her desk and soon finished the note, which she enclosed in an envelope and gave it to Sam.

"Till then," she said. She gripped his hand, and he was gone.

●

Sam patted his Appaloosa as he headed south toward Big Spring. It was approximately two hundred miles to Matt and Bess's home. He found several nice camping areas and arrived in four days.

It was a beautiful day, and the weather was excellent as he rode through the grasslands until he came to the valley, where he could see the TM Ranch. He sat and looked at the beauty of the place and how well repaired were the buildings. Two cowboys came riding to meet him, and each carried a Winchester. They were inquisitive until they found out he was Johnny's brother.

"You're a spitting image of your brother; I'm a cousin to his wife. I'm Eagle Feather," said a tall Indian.

"I'm Andy. I owe my life to your brother, who saved me when an arrow clipped my lung. Our boss will be happy to meet you, Sam," said Andy. "I'll take him on in, Eagle Feather." Sam and Andy rode past barns, paddocks of horses, and cattle to a single-story hacienda that was white washed and had a tiled roof. A woman of extreme beauty was working in a flower garden behind the house. She laid down her hoe, took off a sombrero, and was at the front of the hacienda to meet Andy and Sam as they approached.

"Mrs. McDowell, this is Johnny's brother, Sam," stated Andy.

"I'm glad that you put me straight, Andy, for I was sure that Johnny was here. Sam, welcome to the TM Ranch." She extended her hand and then patted the Appaloosa.

"I can see where Cheryl gets her beauty," smiled Sam.

"You have met my daughter? How is she? We see her so infrequently that it is a privilege to hear from her," stated Mrs. McDowell.

"I saw her four days ago, and she was fine. She wrote this note just as I was leaving. Johnny had a dinner for me the other night so I could meet his inner group, and she was there. She was the life of the party and a very charming lady. This week I had business with her bank. I was impressed how well she knew the banking business," Sam revealed.

"How nice of you, Sam; you have the same charm as your brother, and I hope that you do as well here as Johnny has. Won't you come in? My husband, Tom, is in his office working on books."

A very pretty young lady came to the door as Melody and Sam approached. Sam was stunned at her beauty, for no one had said anything about this girl, and he was amazed. She was as pretty as Cheryl, and both had their mother's beauty and charm.

"I'm Katherine—Katie, to my friends. I've been away to school, and I'm on my break. My brother, Howard, is on his break too and is over at Granddad's place. You have to be Johnny's brother."

"Yes, I'm Samuel—Sam, to my friends," said Sam. *This girl must be about nineteen or twenty,* he thought. *What an extremely beautiful girl she is. She will give Cheryl a lot of competition. I bet this Katie is a heartbreaker.*

A man Sam believed to be in his middle forties walked from his office into the hall. He was graying at his temples, had wide shoulders, a narrow waist, and corduroy trousers, tucked into Texas boots.

"Well, I'll be! You have to be Samuel, Johnny's younger brother. Johnny has been seeking you for years and talked of you often. Welcome to the TM ranch," said Tom McDowell.

"I'm on my way to see Matt and Bess to deliver a deed for Johnny, and Johnny asked me to drop by and say hello to you. Johnny thinks a lot of you and the help you gave him in life. You have such warmth, I can see where he could find happiness here among you folk," stated Sam.

"Your sister has made my son so happy, and we are looking forward to seeing our first grandchild. We are very fond of Nina. She is such a lovely girl," stated Tom.

"Nina is only a year older than I, but when our folks died she took care of me until I got old enough to step up and help us both. I love her as a sister and as a little mother to me also," said Sam.

"Mr. Ragan, please stay for lunch, as I was about ready to have our cook prepare the meal. It isn't far to Matt and Bess's place, but you will need to eat. You drove past it when you came through the valley," declared Mrs. McDowell.

"Thank you so much for the invitation. I believe I will, if it is not too inconvenient. How far is it from here to the Mission?" Sam asked Tom.

"It is about a four-day ride, and I will have Andy ride to our border shacks near the Canadian so you won't get lost. If you do not have a compass, I'll have Andy to loan you one of ours," said Tom.

"That's very kind of you, sir!"

"We have not had any trouble with rustlers since Slim left us, but there is some evidence that they may become active again. The changing over of our currency into silver has caused a lot of panic among common folk. They think they must steal from others to offset the loss of a few dollars. You be careful around those line shacks. Johnny had a Sharp's 1863, 54-caliber rifle, which he was a great marksman with and more than once he punished cattle rustlers while in my employment. You have a lot of reason to be proud of your brother; Johnny saved the life of our cook from drowning and doctored Andy back to life when an arrow clipped his lung. Yes, Johnny holds a very high place in our lives," declared Tom McDowell.

Kate took Sam by the arm and led him to the kitchen to meet the cook. Again, the story was told by the cook of how he almost drowned in the Canadian River in Oklahoma. Sam really liked the cook, for he was a down-to-earth sort of guy. His hair, what was left of it, had turned white, but he was still a good cook and worked hard at his job.

Kate took Sam out to see their horses and paused to admire Sam's Appaloosa. "Can you name him? I've been trying to think of a name for him. I've not had him very long," said Sam as Kate made over the Appaloosa.

"Dad gave my granddad an Appaloosa many years ago and next to my grandmother, Bess, he loves that horse dearly." She laughed.

"I bet that you are held very highly by Mr. Willard and Bess too," spoke up Sam.

"Oh, what a fine thing to say, Sam. I must put you on my very best of friends' list for saying such a thing." She turned her enormous blue eyes on him, and her smile was deep and thankful.

Oh, what a very splendid girl! His thought went to Cheryl for Cheryl was not a child but a very lovely woman. Kate was still immature. *I wonder if she has ever been kissed? Good land! What am I thinking? I just met her an hour ago.* He blushed at his thinking, and Kate noticed.

"Lunch is ready," called Melody. Kate took him by the arm and led him back to the hacienda.

"Oh Dad, you should see Sam's Appaloosa, and he needs a name for him. He asked me if I could name him, but my mind's a blank."

To Sam, she put the question, "Have you seen Johnny's Appaloosa? Has he told you how he got that horse?" asked Kate. "I'm sure that you remembered Jane, Johnny's Grulla that died fighting for him at the Mission. It is such a romantic story of the love of a horse for Johnny," sighed Kate.

"Sit there Sam," directed Tom McDowell. "Kate, honey, you can sit across from Sam." Tom bowed his head and said a prayer for the food. All said, "Amen." The lunch was an excellent meal, and Sam dreaded to leave but was rather anxious about the trip to the Mission. Kate got permission from her dad to ride with Andy and Sam as far as the Willard's. After Sam had left, Tom looked at his wife and said, "I believe that he is the same caliber as his brother, and I'll not stand in his way of him courting my Kate. Don't you think we learned a hard lesson with Cheryl?"

"My husband, Kate is too immature for such a man as Sam. Wouldn't it be something if our unhappy Cheryl and Sam got interested in each other?"

"I never even thought of that. Isn't she older than he? A year, maybe?! Let us put it in the hands of the good Lord. Kate or Cheryl? Boy, what a place for a young man to be! The two most beautiful girls in Texas, and he can make a pick?" smiled Tom.

•

Kate, Andy, and Sam rode into the yard of Bess and Matt Willard. They were the father and mother of Tom's first wife who had been killed in an Indian raid on the hacienda. Matt was a retired Texas ranger, and he and Bess had loved Melody after their daughter had been killed.

Matt and Bess came to the door and stood on the porch while introductions were made. Sam, wishing to hurry along, explained his need to continue his trip. He delivered the deed to Matt of property that Johnny had sold to Matt. He and Andy rode on toward the line shacks, while Kate stood on the porch and waved as long as she could see them.

"I believe that you have made a hit with Kate. Every cowboy on this ranch is in love with her. She is always the same very likeable young lady. She is a senior at Texas Christian College in Fort Worth and home now till school starts in September," drawled Andy.

"There is a Christian Church College in Ft. Worth? I didn't see such a college, but I sure saw a lot of evilness when I was there. I almost lost my life too. I guess that most cities have a good side and an evil one. I saw only the evil side." Sam went on to explain how he was knifed and how William had been imprisoned. Andy just rode and listened.

The river was just ahead so the line shacks must be near, thought Samuel.

They rode into the line shack and found that it had been raided, and the two cowboys that stayed there had been killed. There were unshod tracks galore in front and around the cabin. The cowboys had made a good stand, but there had been too many rustlers.

"I will stay here with the bodies while you ride and get some help. These horses are unshod and it looks like Indian ponies. See how small the hoof is. They are mustangs, I believe," said Sam as he leaned over them.

"It is three now, so I will be back with some help by dark. Watch out, for they may return. Here, take my Winchester and plenty of shells just in case you might need it," said Andy, and then he rode off.

There were some vultures circling over the line shack, so Sam decided to take the bodies into the building. The bodies had been mutilated, scalped, and stripped of clothing. By the time he had finished his chore, he heard firing off to the east. He ventured outside and the sound was plain. *There must be another cabin about a mile to the west . . .* He checked the rifle and approached the sound of gunfire. He tied his Appaloosa to a tree and crawled along a small creek that ran into the Canadian River. Several Indians were near the cabin and were drawing fire from the dwelling. This cabin was a larger building and had a second story, or maybe it had an upstairs attic. The cowboy or cowboys were accurate with their fire for several Indians lay prone in front of the dwelling.

Should Sam hold his fire until Andy got back, or should he add his support to those in the line shack? As he was considering what to do, a brave followed his tracks up the ravine and Sam shot the Indian point black in the middle of his breast. He turned his rifle on those at the side of the line shack. He had killed only a few times, and killing was not coming easy to him. These were Pawnee for he could see their top knots. Most of the Indians had bow and arrows and the sound of his Winchester drew the attention of both the Indians and those inside the line shack. He missed his first two shots but then took his time and became very accurate with the gun. Finally, his location was observed by both Indians and cowboys. The Indians tried to outflank him, and he had to move so that he could get better shots on those coming up the ravine. The cowboys within the house were supporting him, and made it more difficult for the Indians to approach him from his rear. While the cowboys were shooting at those in the ravine, he turned his attention to the Indians at the side of the line shack which the cowboys could not see. He had a clear shot at them and his shooting became very accurate.

Indians ran for their horses, and together they rode toward the Canadian River, toward the West. The door opened and three cowboys cautiously came onto the porch. Sam stood up and he heard one of the cowboys say, "I believe it is Johnny Ragan."

Sam walked toward the line shack but turned and watched down the ravine, lest some Indian was still stalking him from that area.

"Johnny, we were about done in; God sure sent you at the right time. What are you doing way down here? Whoa, that's not Johnny." All three men stood and stared at Sam.

"I'm Sam, brother to Johnny; I heard your firing from the other line shack, and I thought I should try to help. I'm sorry that I have to report, but there are two dead at the other line shack," stated Sam.

"Ah, no!" called one. "Those Pawnee are murderers."

"Look, the cattle in that paddock are still there, and I'm sure they had it in mind to drive them off when they left," stated another cowboy.

"Andy has ridden for help! He should be back in about three hours," Sam said.

"You really put the hurt on those Indians. You have a Winchester like our boss provides for us," said an observant cowboy.

"It is Andy's gun, but he left it for me when he rode for help. Anybody hurt in the shack?" asked Sam.

"They didn't know that we were here, and we saw the dust from their horses and heard the gunfire when they attacked the other line shack. William and Robert dead! That will really hurt little Kate, for I think she and William were seeing one another. What a shame, a guy just does not know when the reaper will call," added another cowboy.

"Sam, I'm George Cavenaugh, and I'm one of the ram rods for the TM Ranch. That guy there is another Sam, Sam Rodgers, and the last one is Roy McEvers. I think I speak for all when I say it was a very pleasant surprise to us, and to the Indians, when you opened up with that rifle. I don't know how the rest of you guys felt, but I was afraid that my time had come. Let's head to the other line shack and wait for the guys to come. I believe the Pawnee stole our horses, but there are some saddles and bridles in the house and we can help ourselves to an Indian pony or two." The three proved they knew horses, for they soon had them tied and saddled.

"Man, I don't see how those Pawnee can ride a poor critter like this horse," complained Sam Rodgers. "Someone must have shot the last rider or this horse's backbone did the trick!"

Darkness was coming fast as the three approached the line shack where their dead friends lay. A lantern was lit and one of the younger cowboys was sick when they saw the condition of the naked men.

"I heard that the Pawnee mutilated the dead, and here is proof. I saw what they did to Erma's husband but they were half-breed Apache," said George.

"They say that scalping originated with the French, during the French and English war, and the French bought scalps. That just isn't civilized," said the young cowboy.

"I hear horses, fellows, get ready—those demons may have come back," opined George.

"Hello, Sam, it's us!" called Andy. A full two dozen cowboys, armed to the teeth, rode up to the porch.

"They have killed young William and Robert too. Boy, do I hate that. Those guys were full of life," said George Cavenaugh. "They might have gotten us too had not Sam here lent a hand. Boss, I believe he is as good a shot as Johnny."

Tom McDowell stood bent over the two dead, young cowboys. Matt Willard, a man who had seen so many dead, was white as death itself.

"I never get use to seeing what an Indian can do to the dead. Just why they do this is anybody's guess; I understand they did this same thing to Custer's whole troop," said Matt.

The entire group was very quiet and respectful to their lost friends. This tight knit group regretted deeply the loss of life. "Those Indians will be in the same area where you will be traveling, Sam. They are on the war path for some reason, and would gang up on you if they saw you. I think you had better stay over at the hacienda for a week and give this time to settle down. George, wrap those boys up and let us take them back in the morning. Those were Pawnee and they may try to dress like wolves and attack our camp tonight. We'll post a guard just in case," stated Tom McDowell. "Sam, thanks for helping out."

The crew settled down to sleep, and there were three guards out around the line shack. Eagle Feather came in from a scouting trip.

"Boss, they came and got their dead during the night and are traveling West in a hurry. They know we are here and have rounded up a few stray horses belonging to their fallen comrades. They are hurt! They really lost several between Sam and the fire from the line shack. William and Robert killed five or maybe six, so this raid will not be forgotten by them."

"Nor by us, either!" whispered Tom.

After a hasty breakfast, Tom McDowell led his small army back to the hacienda. Kate wept sorely and her mother put her to bed. She was a child imprisoned in a woman's body. Emotionally she needed to grow; sometimes it is through hard knocks that this kind of growth is only possible.

Sam knew that Cheryl was the lady that he would pursue when this was all over. The next week was spent in burying William and Robert. Johnny and several of his inner group, who knew the boys well, came to the funeral. Ruth came in a surrey, well-escorted. Cheryl accompanied her and the baby. Sam saw that the entire group was all like brothers and sisters. Nina and William came too, and Nina rode with Ruth and Cheryl; William rode along behind.

Cheryl was distant, but Sam felt it was due to the casual manner he had when around her. She just did not know how to act around Sam. Kate showed affection to Sam in various ways, but Sam treated her like a sister. She was not used to men holding her at a distance, and she was like Cheryl, she did not know what to do. Tom and Melody were watching things from a distance and Tom said to his wife, "Sam is as smart as can be in handling our two girls. I must admit I do not know why Cheryl is holding Sam at arm's length. I can see that Cheryl is a bit disgusted at Kate's throwing herself at Sam. Sam sees Kate as being immature and looks often to see what Cheryl is doing. I believe Sam is interested in our Cheryl. In the fight at the Line Cabins, Sam really conducted himself in a mature, deadly manner. He is very much a mature man and as strong as an ox."

"Oh Tom, we must stay out of this and not take sides. Cheryl just needs a man to reassure her after the Johnny fiasco. Let us pray for her and Sam too, that the good Lord might step in and love may prevail," stated Melody.

•

The McDowell graveyard was growing and the wrought-iron fence had been enlarged. Melody kept fresh flowers on the graves, but only she and Kate ventured there.

A week after the battle at the Line Shacks and, following the funerals, Sam took a compass and rode out on his way to the Mission. He had company as far as Amarillo and stayed at Johnny's for one night. He spent no time with Cheryl and had no difficulty in finding the mission field and the reservation. Ruth had sent a letter with him to her folks.

John Beasley saw him coming, and thought at first that it was Johnny. He called Causes to Laugh, and he and his wife stood on the front porch where they awaited their son-in-law. As Sam was almost on them, they saw that it was not Johnny, and wondered who this stranger could be. Sam rode to the porch and introduced himself. He had a letter of introduction from Johnny telling the reason for Johnny being there. A smile crossed John Beasley's face as he learned why Sam had come.

"Sam here wants to teach farriery and wagon construction to our tribe. This will give us another means of livelihood to teach our people. I feel that there will be a keen interest in shoeing horses and working at a forge. Welcome Sam! How are Ruth and the little one? Johnny okay?" asked John. Sam produced the letter that Ruth had written.

Sam noticed the extreme beauty of Causes to Laugh and she had a wonderful spirit in her heart and life. "Ben, take Mr. Ragan to meet Red Hand, for he will be a guest of the tribe. Sam, Red Hand is a half-brother to my wife," declared John Beasley.

Sam followed Ruth's brother, Ben, to Red Hand's wigwam and introductions were made.

"So you are the brother of the great hunter, Johnny. I saw him kill a deer about as far as a soul can see. Johnny is a great medicine man too. I gave him my horse for saving our tribe from the Pawnee," said Red Hand, smiling.

"I've seen his horse, and it is a good one! I have one that is like it. My horse was given to me by Big Beaver, the scout. Big Beaver told me that his tribe raises Appaloosa. Big Beaver belongs to the Nez Perce tribe; Joseph was their chief," stated Sam.

Red Hand had a faraway look in his eyes, and then he turned to Sam. "I know Big Beaver, for he brought the Appaloosa that I gave to Johnny as a gift to my father, and when I became a man, my father gave it to me. Your brother fought the Pawnee and kept them from raiding and stealing our women. He lost his horse and I gave him the best gift that I had, my Appaloosa. Johnny is a great warrior and lives in a big wigwam. Please stay with us many moons, and teach our people how to put round rings on horses' hoofs." Sam walked back to the mission, where Causes to Laugh was preparing the evening meal.

Ben was a fine young man with red hair like his dad's. He was taking on some of the traits of an Indian, for he did not have much to say. Red Hand was very fond of his nephew and was looking forward to initiating him into the manhood of the tribe, but that was a problem with John and Causes to Laugh.

●

Dinner was served, and John Beasley prayed for the food. After the evening meal, while Causes to Laugh washed the dishes, Sam and John sat in the parlor, and John told Sam, in great detail, about the trouble that Ruth had with Johnny. The missionary told how Causes to Laugh and he had prayed that God's will be done, and Johnny and Ruth had found each other again and had remarried. Ruth had no problem conceiving and carrying to term their child. A tear was in the missionary's eye when he finished.

"The Lord is so good to us all." Sam bowed his head, as he knew that John Beasley was praying a prayer of thanksgiving. Sam realized that he was in the presence of a man who deeply believed in Christ.

"Red Hand told me that you had trouble with the Pawnee, and Johnny fought for the tribe. A week or so ago the TM Ranch lost two cowboys up at the Line Shacks. I was in the battle and for the second time in my life, I killed men. I can't get it out of my mind, and it bothers me at night. I shot to save three cowboys who were trapped in one of the houses. I think of those savages when I should be sleeping, but I had to help those men. The savages were Pawnee and I fought for my life."

"You know, Johnny had the same problem when he was here, for he had killed rustlers, as I remember it, and it was bothering his conscience too. I told him that the Hebrew, used in the Ten Commandments meant, Thou shall not commit murder. Johnny and I agreed that Johnny was fighting to save lives just as a man does in the army. He saved our Ruth and warned Red Hand that the Pawnee were near. Johnny killed to save lives just as you did." Sam thought about it for a while, and knew he would sleep better in the future.

"Come, it is near chapel time. Do you sing as well as Johnny does?" asked John.

"I had no idea that Johnny could sing. I'll not be known for my singing, as I only sing when I bathe," said Sam.

After chapel, John introduced Sam to the adult group and to a great helper, a teacher by the name of Thomas C. Battery. Mr. Battery was very interested in Sam teaching a course in wagon making and blacksmith work.

"This will greatly aid our men in another profession," said Mr. Battery. Six of the men agreed to take the course, and Sam began the next day. He set up his forge and shoed several horses while answering questions from his class. In the afternoon, he began to make a wagon which drew the attention of Red Hand and other Elders of the clan. For six months Sam taught and built, until he could leave Mr. Battery in charge of the new class. Six of the class were asked to go to Amarillo, to go to work for Sam. It was amazing how fast they'd learned.

•

Sam rode the hundred twenty-five miles to Amarillo and stopped at Johnny's office, where he introduced his Indian employees to Johnny. While Sam was at the Mission, Johnny had William build a shop and a large permanent forge. Sam wanted to see Cheryl, so he stopped by the bank and questioned Cheryl what the cost of construction was so he could recompense Johnny.

"Johnny has never said anything about you paying for the construction. You will have to ask him." She looked him straight in the eyes and smiled.

"Oh by the way, I've missed you and welcome back." The door to the office was closed, so he took her in his arms. She trembled as he kissed her tenderly.

"Sam, I needed that so much." She sighed.

"Cheryl, I feel that I love you, but is your love for me, or do you care yet for Johnny?" asked Sam, and he watched her carefully as she considered an answer.

"Sam, I was the one who lost Johnny, and it nearly broke my heart. I was angry at first, then bitter, then I cried a lot. But when little Naomi was born, I knew I was wrong and what Johnny had done was right. He loved Ruth! Time has helped me, and then you came along. God must have sent you, for I see in you an answer to all my problems."

"Cheryl, I love you, honey. Eventually I want you as my wife, but I need a business and a home to call our own. We need to give this some more time; 'till death do us part'—now that is a long, long time. I also want to get right with God. I believe in Christ and his lovely teachings and want them as the center of my life. May we trust completely His teachings? John Beasley really preached to me when I was at the Mission."

"Oh Samuel, what you say has made my heart glad." She moved into his arms, and the kiss she gave was full of love and care. It was like her immortal soul delivered it. He held her very closely and knew that her kiss was for him and him only. From that time forward they knew that she was for him and he was for her. They were together constantly. He bought her an engagement ring, which only increased her happiness.

Sam and his crew of Kiowa worked hard on wagons, buggies, and surreys; as the population of Texas grew, more and more people were drawn to the panhandle of Texas. The rent continued to arrive from Oklahoma, and Sam widened his business, especially his wagons and buggies, to several towns and cities. Sam and Johnny became known as The Ragan Brothers. Johnny helped Sam get involved in more commerce, and Sam spread his business ventures into Oklahoma City, especially into real estate, for the business area widened and spread south and overlapped his real estate and the lands that Jon had bought. His venture into real estate was widened into Fort Worth and a small town called Monterey, Texas. Sam had passed the town as he headed north toward Amarillo. It was a dusty little town, but Sam bought several farms in and around the town, believing that some day it might grow into a good venture. Old Lubbock united with Monterey and became known as Lubbock, Texas, in 1890.

•

When Big Beaver left Samuel, he greatly prized the rifle that Sam had given to him. He also felt a vast kinship for the blacksmith and gave him one of his Appaloosa mares. Big Beaver was of the Nez Perce tribe, and they honored highly the Appaloosa horse, so much so that they looked on the animal as a god. Whenever a warrior lost his life, whether from disease or battle, his personal animal, his Appaloosa, was slain and its head, tail, and hoofs were cut off and put on display at the grave of the warrior.

The Nez Perce tribe was from the Wallowa Valley, near the Snake River, where Idaho, Oregon, and Washington meet. It was led by a chief named Hinmahtooyahlahtket and became known as Chief Joseph, after his dad, who had been named by a missionary. Young Joseph wanted peace with the white man and tried to live in a peaceful way with them. He had no love for the reservation but simply wanted to be left alone. When other tribes joined the reservation, the Nez Perce let their hair grow long, out of disdain for the white man, and the reservation Indians, who cut their hair short. The tribe was greatly angered when white settlers raided the Nez Perce village and managed to steal about a thousand of the prize Appaloosa horses.

In a battle with the U.S. Cavalry at White Bird Creek, the Nez Perce tribe slaughtered thirty-four of Perry's soldiers and lost only two of their warriors. The Indians picked up several guns from the battlefield and managed to keep away from a Gatling Gun the soldiers used for greater fire power.

Chief Joseph moved his tribe from the mountains and attempted to enter the plains to the east of Montana. In the Lolo Pass, the army had constructed a fort to prevent such a maneuver. Chief Joseph surrounded the fort, which was manned by thirty-five regulars of the seventh infantry division, as well as two hundred militia volunteers. He let it be known that all he wanted was access to the plains. The personnel in the fort backed down, and the name of the fort was changed to "Fort Fizzle." The Nez Perce tribe sought the safety of the plains. This history had happened before Big Beaver's trip to San Antonio.

On December 29th, 1890, Big Beaver, with a half dozen Appaloosa horses, was camped south of Wounded Knee Creek,

South Dakota. His hair was long, and his person unclean from weeks of camping and attempting to hide from the military.

The Seventh Cavalry, with 365 troops, supported by four Hotchkiss guns, had surrounded an encampment of Lakota Sioux. The Sioux were cornered and had agreed to turn themselves in at the Pine Ridge Agency at Omaha, Nebraska. The Seventh Calvary was there to disarm the warriors and see to it that the Sioux fulfilled that agreement.

During the disarmament, a deaf warrior who could not hear the order to disarm refused to give up his weapon, which caused the soldiers to fire on the warriors, women, and children alike, as well as some of their own troopers. When it was all over, 146 men, women, and children were dead, and twenty-five troopers also lost their lives.

Big Beaver heard the fire and fled southward, pushing his Appaloosa ahead of him. Where could he find refuge? Where would be drive his horses? He thought of his friend, Sam Ragan, and turned his horses toward Amarillo, three hundred miles to the south.

●

Cheryl asked Sam to come to her office. "Honey, I have been going over your account, and do you know that you are almost as rich as Johnny? The growth of your real estate and your buggy business has made you one of the richest men in northern Texas. I would like for you to marry me! I want children, and I want them while we are young and can enjoy them. I do not want a huge house; I would even settle for a small ranch. I am also to the place where I would like to quit banking and just become a full-time wife. Sam, let us get married and start working at producing children."

Sam took her into his arms. "That is the best proposal that I have ever had." He smiled. "When do you want to do this? I'm very willing."

"I do not want a big marriage, just some of my friends," she said.

"Set the date and away we go!"

"How about three weeks from Saturday? It will let me get a dress, send a few invitations, and then give Johnny my two weeks' notice. I'm going into this married life full time, so you can expect for us to be parents as soon as possible. Prior to the marriage vow, I want us both to be baptized and make a full-time commitment to Christ."

"I agree!" said Sam.

The marriage was planned small, but Cheryl just couldn't invite this one, or that one, and not invite someone else. Kate, Nina, and Ruth, were all included in her wedding, as maids of honor, bridesmaids, etc. Ushers galore were included. There were cowboys, Indians, and various men of different professions. All were invited, and all came. Sam asked John Beasley to conduct the wedding and John baptized Cheryl and Sam just a week before the nuptials were read.

A very happy couple, spiritually clean, and very much in love, said their vows and made their promises to each other. Melody Mc Dowell whispered to her husband as the ceremonial ended. "Isn't it wonderful how God has worked this out? They are made for each other. Our daughter is so happy!"

Johnny was best man and stood by his brother and watched Cheryl make her vows. What an extremely beautiful bride she was.

They honeymooned for a week, and then over breakfast one morning, talked about a future home. "Do you want to stay here in Amarillo?" asked Sam. She studied a moment and sipped her coffee.

"Sam, I'd like to live near my granddad and grandmother, Roy and Bess Willard. I want to be near my mom and dad and the hacienda. That place will always be home to me. Can we find such a place to raise our children?"

"Honey, anywhere down in that area would be fine with me. The railroad will be bringing in a lot of neighbors; let us see just where we can buy."

•

Eagle Feather was scouting north of Amarillo, near to the Canadian River. He was well hidden as he watched a lone Indian watering a string of horses. The horses were Appaloosa and were a rare breed to be found in this area. Eagle Feather rose up from behind the rock where he was hiding and lifted his hand as a sign of peace. He had found Big Beaver, who was trying to find Sam. Eagle Feather took Big Beaver to Sam.

"Why do you not wear the short hair of an Army scout? Do you not believe as they do?" asked Eagle Feather.

"I have let my hair grow long out of contempt for the military. I have lost all of my family," explained Big Beaver. "The Army has killed all of the women and children and they seek to kill me, for I have fought them and will till they kill me. I have six bred Appaloosa mares and as far as I know they are the last of the horses of the Nez Perce Wallowa Tribe. I am at a loss as to where I can go, for the army knows where I have sought refuge in the past. I am very weary, for my journey has been long."

"I work for the Ragan brothers. I believe that you have met Samuel for he speaks of you often, and rides with pride the horse that you gave him," said Eagle Feather. "Sam has married, but is still at Amarillo. He is making plans to move south, just north of Big Spring. You two need to talk, for he will give you refuge and a place to work. Make camp here where the water is good; I will bring Sam to you." The agreement was made and Eagle Feather found Sam and brought him to Big Beaver.

Before the scout asked Sam for refuge, Sam offered him a home and a place where he would be safe.

"I have at last found peace, and Sam, my friend, I long to have roots and a place to grow old. Sam, you are the only white man that I know who can help me find such peace."

"Eagle Feather and I have the 'peace that passeth understanding,' but it comes in a very special way. We will tell you how to find such peace."

Eagle Feather grinned. "I will tell him. I have found the giver of life."

EPILOGUE

When Cheryl told Matt and Bess of their desire to live near them, Matt and Bess were delighted. "We have an extra house and land that used to belong to Johnny and Ruth. It was their honeymoon cottage and the house was constructed by the cowboys of the TM ranch. Johnny sold it to us when Ruth left him. The house is vacant now and needs cleaning and some care. It is a pale green with double hung windows and an excellent hip roof. The front porch looks out over our valley!" Matt took Sam aside and told Sam that he was near to seventy in age. Ranching was getting the best of him, and he would like to retire.

"Sam, will you take charge of my thousand-acre ranch?" The offer greatly impressed and pleased Sam, and he agreed to help Matt and told Matt of Big Beaver.

"I'll buy Big Beaver's mares and hire him to be my foreman, for I know of no person who knows more about horses, especially the strain of horses that you and I love. He is a good Indian and needs a family," stated Sam.

Sam paid cash for the house and added a few improvements, but not without questioning Cheryl if it made any difference who were the former owners.

"All of that is in the past! Sam, I love you with all my heart, and this is a good place to raise our children." Cheryl soon gave birth to twin boys, Aidan and Gavan. The boys were dark complexioned, and had dark hair like their dad. Sam and Cheryl raised them in the Lord and had a lot of help from Granddad Tom McDowell and Grandmother Melody McDowell. Matt and Bess were close to give advice, as well as twenty TM cowboys. Cheryl had a little girl with blue eyes and light brown hair. Sam and Cheryl named her Catherine and called her Cathy. She was a beautiful child. "Just like her mother," declared Sam.

Kate had several boyfriends, for she was such a beautiful girl. She met Ben Beasley on a trip to the mission and was enchanted by his red head. He talked very little but one day got up enough nerve to ask her to marry him. They were married by John Beasley and eventually took over the work at the mission.

Johnny and Ruth had two additional sons, and Ruth gave praise to her God, because she carried them all to term.

•

Sam constructed a church building between his house and Matt and Bess's home. Near to the house of God, he constructed a parsonage. To his delight, he received a letter from John and Causes to Laugh, telling of their retirement from the mission and turning over the mission work to their son, Ben, and Kate. Would the new congregation be interested in a worn out missionary as their first minister? Sam hurried with the letter to the new congregation, and John was hired.

Sam became an elder in the new church, along with Matt and Tom. Deacons came from cowboys of the TM Ranch. Newcomers in the area attended and sought the Lord in great numbers. There is nothing so thrilling as seeing people seek His name!

Ben became a great preacher, and Kate put to work what she learned in college at Texas Christian University. The mission grew and prospered.

•

William Slovic served three years and four months at hard labor, but the term taught him nothing. He made himself a sap and used it several times to steal what he could. An Apache renegade sidestepped one of his attempts, and stuck a homemade knife between his second and third rib. The knife penetrated his heart and with his last breath he cursed the very one whom he would meet when he breathed his last. "It is appointed unto man, once to die, and after this the judgment" (Hebrews 9:27, KJV).

•

Slim Wilkins married Mildred Wilson, a brunette girl from Amarillo, and Johnny had a home built for Slim and Mildred by William McDowell. The inner group continued in love and fellowship and remained tight knit and in unity.

•

William built a fancy barn behind Sam's house, and Sam planned his Appaloosa herd. Sam used Johnny's, Matt's, and his own stallions for studs. The horse herd grew and the ranch prospered. Aidan and Gavan were raised as horsemen and were either with Sam, Matt, or Big Beaver around their beloved Appaloosa horses. Cheryl often went riding with her boys and had her own Appaloosa mare.

Cathy, with her light brown hair and large, blue eyes, played havoc with the next generation of TM cowboys.

•

Ben and Kate had two boys and two girls. The boys were red headed and loved to visit with their uncle Red Hand. The two girls were spitting images of their beautiful mother. The mission was in good hands and continued to grow. The Ragan brothers were among the main contributors to the work.

•

Big Beaver met Marie, who was the eldest daughter of Amos and Red Doe. Amos had named his daughter Marie after the mother of Jesus, which was a common name among the French. The girl had her mother's charm and Indian ways. Her hair was black, and she was pretty in manner as well as in form. Big Beaver brought four of his Appaloosa mares and courted her after the Indian manner. Big Beaver wasn't interested in a lodge of his tribe, but Sam built them a nice cottage for his foreman and they lived near Matt and Bess. Red Hand often came to visit and their friendship flourished. Eventually they became brothers in the church.

•

The Ragan Brothers became well known in the panhandle of Texas. Their honesty and fair dealings with their customers made them prime businessmen. When the need for wagons and buggies slackened, Sam got into Ford products and sold the Model "T" as well as Model "A and B's" along with Ford trucks. The mechanical products were second to Sam's beloved Appaloosa.

And so life continued north of Big Spring.